There was hunger in his gaze. Lust.

"We have a lot in common, Grace." He smiled. "And not only because we're shifters."

She had managed to control the desire she felt whenever she was with Simon. But now, her passion flared, as if it had suddenly burst into flame.

Impulsively, she reached up—and she was suddenly in Simon's arms.

His lips met hers, claiming them. His tongue penetrated her mouth, entering into a sexy duel that made her knees weak.

His scent was raw and masculine and hypnotic. His body was hard and skilled. His growls and sexy rumbles were as wild as their feral natures.

But she knew once he took her to bed, there would be no turning back.

LINDA O. JOHNSTON

loves to write. More than one genre at a time? That's part of the fun. While honing her writing skills, she started working in advertising and public relations, then became a lawyer…and still enjoys writing contracts. Linda's first published fiction novel appeared in *Ellery Queen's Mystery Magazine* and won a Robert L. Fish Memorial Award for Best First Mystery Short Story of the Year. It was the beginning of her versatile fiction-writing career. Linda now spends most of her time creating memorable tales of paranormal romance and mystery.

Linda lives in the Hollywood Hills with her husband and two Cavalier King Charles spaniels. Visit her at her website, www.LindaOJohnston.com.

GUARDIAN WOLF
LINDA O. JOHNSTON

TORONTO NEW YORK LONDON
AMSTERDAM PARIS SYDNEY HAMBURG
STOCKHOLM ATHENS TOKYO MILAN MADRID
PRAGUE WARSAW BUDAPEST AUCKLAND

Recycling programs
for this product may
not exist in your area.

ISBN-13: 978-0-373-61865-1

GUARDIAN WOLF

Copyright © 2011 by Linda O. Johnston

All rights reserved. Except for use in any review, the reproduction or utilization of this work in whole or in part in any form by any electronic, mechanical or other means, now known or hereafter invented, including xerography, photocopying and recording, or in any information storage or retrieval system, is forbidden without the written permission of the publisher, Harlequin Enterprises Limited, 225 Duncan Mill Road, Don Mills, Ontario M3B 3K9, Canada.

This is a work of fiction. Names, characters, places and incidents are either the product of the author's imagination or are used fictitiously, and any resemblance to actual persons, living or dead, business establishments, events or locales is entirely coincidental.

This edition published by arrangement with Harlequin Books S.A.

For questions and comments about the quality of this book please contact us at Customer_eCare@Harlequin.ca.

® and TM are trademarks of the publisher. Trademarks indicated with ® are registered in the United States Patent and Trademark Office, the Canadian Trade Marks Office and in other countries.

www.Harlequin.com

Printed in U.S.A.

Dear Reader,

Guardian Wolf is the third full-length novel about Alpha Force, a highly covert military unit comprised of shape-shifters. It features Lieutenant Grace Andreas, M.D., an Alpha Force member—and shape-shifter—who is sent to an Arizona military hospital on a special assignment. There, she runs into Dr. Simon Parran, the man she once loved. A man who'd hidden from her the fact that he was also a shifter.

I enjoyed writing about their mutual suspicions, emotional baggage…and hot sex life! How easy is it for two werewolves to hide what they are from each other, and everyone else, while both attempting, for their own reasons, to stop the thefts of some highly dangerous biohazards? Throw in a fiery attraction they can't deny, and that's *Guardian Wolf!*

I hope you enjoy the story. Please come visit me at my website, www.LindaOJohnston.com and at my blog, KillerHobbies.blogspot.com. And, yes, I'm on Facebook, too.

Linda O. Johnston

Thanks to Dr. Ken Zangwill for ideas about some of
the diseases referenced in *Guardian Wolf*.
Of course, I approached the plot fictionally,
and any inaccuracies are due to my imagination,
in the interest of enhancing the story.

As always, this book is dedicated to my husband,
Fred, who enjoys that sometimes
wild imagination of mine!

Prologue

No way. It can't be her.

That was Dr. Simon Parran's first reaction as he moved uncomfortably in his seat in the medical center's small, crowded auditorium.

His second was to visualize Grace Andreas in his mind. That gorgeous face with her high cheekbones, full, inviting lips—and soft brown eyes that flashed each time she asked a question. Too many incisive questions, nearly all about him. Questions he wouldn't answer. That had been the problem, back then.

"Lt. Andreas is a physician," continued Colonel Nelson Otis, M.D., the commanding officer at the renowned and well-regarded military hospital where Simon worked. Speaking into a microphone, he stood at the podium at the front of the room, clad in a lab jacket like most of the staff here, including Simon. "Her specialty is infectious diseases."

Simon wouldn't have guessed the Grace he'd known would go into the military—if this was her. But her specialty made sense. Not only because Grace gave a damn about people—or at least she used to—but she was also prone to take on any cause and fight till she won, no matter how badly the odds were stacked against her.

Almost any cause.

Okay, what if this was the Grace Andreas he had known for a short, intense while, during their early pre-med studies in Michigan? He didn't need to do more than be civil to her. No chance of avoiding her, though. He was an infectious diseases specialist, too.

"With Dr. Andreas will be a nurse, Sgt. Kristine Norwood," the commander continued.

Most doctors and other medical staff had gathered in the lecture hall at Charles Carder Medical Center near Phoenix, Arizona, for the short, monthly update about pending matters at the facility. One item always covered was the frequent comings and goings of staff members.

Because the hospital was a military facility,

the fluidity of personnel was a fact of life. Most of the time, Simon didn't care one way or the other.

This time was different.

Well, even if he couldn't help seeing Grace during her tour of duty here, it wasn't like he didn't think of her a lot anyway, despite the passage of so many years since they'd last been together.

But what if she was still as inquisitive as she'd been back then? His primary reason for being here, his secret experiments, were finally beginning to pay off. They were the direct result of who and what he was—and the information he had refused to admit to Grace, no matter how hard she had pressed him. She had hinted more than once that she was like him, making it look as if it shouldn't matter if he disclosed everything.

So had those SOBs who'd feigned unity and friendliness with his family—till they had run amok and killed two close relatives.

If it was *his* Grace, she might try to repeat the past. It wouldn't matter. He was older. Things didn't bother him as much as they had back then. He had learned many ways of protecting himself, his family, their friends.

Now, if she dug in, demanding answers in her sweet but unyielding way, he could laugh it off more easily. Better yet, turn it on her, since she had hinted of her own secrets. Threaten to harm her and her career by reporting her harassment via official military channels. Not that he'd carry through, of course, unless he could do it in a way that wouldn't invite more questions.

Yet…hell. It came to Simon suddenly, in a surge of awareness that nearly made him stand despite being in the middle of a crowded row.

Her timing could hardly be worse. It would be one thing to deal with her almost any day of the month.

But tomorrow night—the night of the day she was arriving?

There would be a full moon. And he had plans.

Chapter 1

Freedom!

Yet potential danger, too. Her control was less this night than most times while shifted.

She reveled in it.

Now, with unleashed pleasure, she ran beneath the full moon in territory unknown and vast. She inhaled unfamiliar, tantalizing scents of the desert, where military aircraft landed in the distance, and buildings filled with people squatted nearby.

Around her were yuccas and cacti and gritty sand beneath her paws. Coolness, because it was night.

All illuminated by the round, gleaming moon.

She had been in this area for hours, alone and out of the way. Pacing in her cherished wildness, yet not going far. It was long into the night now. The risk of being seen by people, even on hospital property, was smaller. She ached to release even more pent-up energy. Her last shift had been more than a week ago.

But she was not here for pleasure.

She had viewed her target before, a special building not far from where she stood. Now she needed to observe it with her heightened senses.

Wolfen senses.

She sought out an opening in the fence between the air force base and military hospital. She slipped through to the medical side, careful to test the scents in the air, listen, ensure she remained alone. Her aide, nearby, would not follow.

The texture beneath her paws turned hard, uneven, warm—a paved road. She loped carefully at the edge so as not to be spotted in moonlight, toward the far border of the parking lot.

She stopped abruptly as she neared the building. The scent—another wolf like her?

Or a feral, nonshifting wolf? Perhaps. But why would it contain a hint of something so familiar? So...alluring?

She waited, still testing the air with her keen senses. Listening. Hearing nothing out of the ordinary. Watching the building surrounded by concealing foliage and shadows. No movement anywhere around.

Too uneasy to approach further, she slowly returned toward where she had crossed from one property to the other.

She inched along the fence on the air force–base side, reaching an area in which shrubbery between the sites was thick.

And waited. Soon, a hint of light over the horizon signaled dawn—and the waning of the full moon's power. Ready? Yes. Pleased? No.

She felt the tugging at her skin, her insides, that warned of her next shift. Her aide would seek her now, to ensure that, while most vulnerable, she was in no danger.

As the pulling and aches increased, she glanced back through the fence.

And saw what she had anticipated, lurking among parked cars in the large hospital parking lot, not far from the now-distant storage building.

A canine form. Another wolf?

Her change took over then, hurting, not unbearably, but inevitably intense.

It would be over soon.

* * *

In a short while, Lt. Grace Andreas, M.D., hunched along the edge of the sand on Zimmer Air Force Base near the fence separating it from Charles Carder Medical Center. She had been sent to the renowned military hospital on her latest mission for Alpha Force, the covert special ops force to which she belonged.

Her knees were bent, her back arched, as she inhaled deeply with her human senses.

She was still nude, and the cool breeze tickled her bare skin. Her assigned aide, Sgt. Kristine Norwood, would catch up soon, with her clothing.

But—with special thanks to the elixir developed by Alpha Force—Grace recalled well the near-human sights and sounds and emotions that engulfed her while in wolfen form.

Including the scent she had smelled near the building at the far edge of the medical center property—the site where, she'd been told, the biohazard materials taken from patients were stored temporarily until incinerated. The site where security was heightened and armed guards were always present, at least in the room adjoining the storage area. The site she had needed to check out, even cursorily, upon her arrival, while in both forms. It was the heart of her mission.

A canine had begun prowling there in the parking lot, most likely a wolf. Another shape-shifter? One not part of Alpha Force?

Dawn had now overtaken the area. She carefully edged along the air-base side of the fence, staying in shadows, especially since she remained unclothed. Other Alpha Force members had altered the base's security cameras in this vicinity. She would not be photographed.

She wanted—no, needed—to see the storage building from this angle, too.

There. Another gap between some of the non-native, well-watered hedge plants—not much, but enough for her to view the hospital property.

The scent she had inhaled before still seemed to fill the air. She was aware of it even in human form, partly thanks to her enhanced senses.

She looked through foliage and fencing, and saw movement on the other side, a distance from where she crouched. Too far for her to be sure, but the glimpse of something—flesh, or perhaps light-colored clothing—from between cars suggested a person, not a wolf.

One who had just shifted, like her, as daybreak arrived?

She couldn't see the person at all now. But the scent. It had been very like one she had known a long time ago, though never in shifted form. Perhaps its owner had not, in fact, been a shifter.

She must be imagining that scent. But why now?

Why, after all these years, did she believe she inhaled the musky, enticing aroma of the man she might have loved long ago, had he been what she suspected—and honest about it?

The person she had glimpsed so briefly, in the distance, was surely not Simon Parran.

"This wasn't where we planned to meet," hissed Sgt. Kristine Norwood. Grace's aide held a blanket around her while handing her a backpack filled with clothing.

"You're right," Grace agreed, observing Kristine's struggle with Bailey, her dog, who tugged on his leash, straining toward the fence.

"Sit, Bailey," Kristine ordered. The well-trained shepherd-Doberman mix obeyed, but Grace could see his eagerness to get through the fence. He must have smelled the same scent Grace had, with his permanently enhanced canine senses. Of course her senses were better than most humans', especially right after a shift. But at the moment Kristine, acting like a mother hen—which was her duty—seemed oblivious.

Kristine was in her late twenties, with short,

raven-black hair and a strong yet attractive chin that complemented her no-nonsense attitude. In addition to being a non-commissioned officer in the U.S. Army, she was a nurse.

Most important, like Grace, she was a member of Alpha Force.

Unlike Grace, she wasn't a shapeshifter. Her mission was to watch Grace's back, in whatever situation, whatever form, Grace found herself. Like last night, and this morning.

"Sorry." Grace finished pulling up her jeans. "I sensed something interesting over by the storage building. I'm still not sure what— who—it was."

Kristine regarded her with piercing brown eyes. "Bailey growled when we were near there a little while ago, but I didn't see anything. Some guy was wandering around the area earlier, though, after dark. I saw him in the moonlight. I kept Bailey and me way back like you wanted so you could do your special form of recon on the area. Was it the thief?"

"I don't know," Grace said slowly. She couldn't believe she'd sensed who she'd thought she had. She'd never forgotten Simon but, even as often as she still thought of him, he'd never appeared in her imagination that way before.

Only in her dreams.

Somehow, she had to find out more about

that wolf. More important, she had to learn who the person was whom she'd seen, and why he'd been so close to the biohazards storage facility. Logic suggested it was the thief.

Were the two beings one and the same? She'd caught only one scent from this distance.

As if hearing her thoughts, Kristine said, "Well, you'd better find out who it is and why he was there—preferably before we call Major Connell."

Major Drew Connell was Grace's superior officer in Alpha Force. He would expect them to report in soon about how things were going—especially after last night's full moon.

"I agree, but it won't happen immediately." Grace strode off toward the residential quarters near the entrance to the air force base where Kristine and she, and the other visiting Alpha Force members, were staying while on this mission.

"When do you have to report for duty at the hospital today?" Kristine asked. "Do you have time for a nap?"

She could take the time but didn't want to. "I'll just walk Tilly, then shower and change clothes," she told Kristine. Tilly, a German shepherd mix, was her cover dog—one who resembled her in shifted form. If anyone ever saw Grace while she was wolfen, she could laugh it off, say they'd seen Tilly. She had been left in Grace's room last night and would need some TLC this morning.

They had reached the boxy, five-story residential building. Other military folks poured out, apparently ready to start the day at the base. Grace and Kristine waited, not wanting to buck the crowd. They received a few curious nods and other greetings, but neither was in uniform and no one saluted them.

Soon, as fewer people were exiting, the two used their key cards and went inside.

"I'll call you when I'm ready to go to the hospital," Grace told Kristine, and headed for her apartment.

Grace knew she should be exhausted. Instead, she was full of nervous energy.

Rather than a walk, she took Tilly out for a jog. There was a running track near the front of the base, where most living quarters were located. They were alone at this hour. Fortunately, although the Arizona day promised to be a hot one, the temperature was bearable for exercise.

When they returned to their quarters, Grace fed Tilly and ensured she had sufficient water, then took a shower and dressed. Adrenaline had awakened her enough to face the day.

That, and the intriguing identity of the stranger near the biohazard storage last night. Two beings, a wolf and a man?

And by some odd happenstance, could either have been Simon Parran?

She had seen no indication last night of anyone staking out the storage facility for potential thieves. Unless, of course, that was the intent of the person she had glimpsed so near dawn and so briefly. Or the person Kristine had seen just after sunset. He, at least, couldn't have been a shifter, since they all changed as the full moon rose in the darkness of night.

A lot to check into.

As promised, she called Kristine. "You awake?"

The sergeant muttered something, then said, "Of course."

"Take your time. In an hour or so, you can go back to the investigation you started yesterday. I'll want you to bring Tilly to the hospital for therapy visits this afternoon. Meantime, get some rest." Kristine wasn't reporting for nurse duty until tomorrow.

"Yes, ma'am," her aide said crisply, humor in her tone. "I'll get an extra forty winks for you, too."

Smiling, Grace called the medical center–commander's office. She learned from his secretary that he would squeeze her in first thing that morning.

After donning white hospital scrubs and attractive yet comfortable rubber-soled shoes, she left for the hospital next door. On arrival, she stopped in a doctor's lounge she'd seen yesterday, grabbed a spare medical jacket from its supply of extras, and pinned onto it the name tag she'd been given.

The medical-center building was vast and smelled of antiseptics overlying odors of wounds and disease. As Grace hurried through the halls, she glanced at the faces of people she passed. She recognized a few she'd met yesterday, but their scents were not the one she had smelled in last night's moonlight.

In a few minutes, she arrived at the commander's office.

"Have a seat, Lieutenant." Colonel Nelson Otis waved in the direction of the chairs facing his gray metal desk, where file folders were stacked in six neat piles. Like Grace, he was both a military officer and a medical doctor.

"Thank you, sir." Grace sat down.

Colonel Otis was a large man, also dressed in a white lab jacket. His face was round, his gray hair a stubble that started halfway back on his head. He sat behind the desk in his large, military-pristine office, regarding her so intensely over half-glasses that she felt uncomfortable.

But she regarded him right back with an unwavering stare. She had long ago learned to deal with people who attempted to intimidate her for no reason other than to stroke their egos. She had to be careful with her attitude, now that she was in the military, but in most Alpha Force situations, she fortunately did not have to impress the brass to whom she ostensibly reported. Her real commanding officers were on the East Coast, at Ft. Lukman on Maryland's Eastern Shore.

On the other hand, she had to get along with folks on her missions, especially egotistical military sorts. She made herself look away first.

"What did you think of your first day here yesterday, Lieutenant?" the colonel asked. "Did you find out who our thief is?"

She doubted he would be so sarcastic with a man in her position. He of course had no idea of her special abilities, or why she was much better qualified to find the missing hazardous substances than almost any other member of the military.

He certainly didn't know how she had patrolled the air base and medical center last night.

"Not yet, sir. But I will."

"Don't get overconfident," he snapped. "I've had not only local military security but also investigators from the U.S. Air Force Office of Special Investigations check things out, and they found nothing definitive. Because of the sensitive nature of what's being stolen, and the need for a quick resolution, I asked for additional help—and they had you and your buddies assigned to Zimmer. But none of you seems the kind to figure this out fast. A medical doctor, a flight communications officer and some NCOs—who the hell are you?"

"We're members of Alpha Force, Colonel." Grace knew that the pride that came through in her tone would only irritate him more. "I know you've been told we're a covert special ops force, sir." If he only knew how special...

"But nothing more about you," he asserted belligerently. He was aware, though, that all Alpha Force members who had been sent for this assignment were women, which undoubtedly factored into his attitude. He seemed all old-school military to her.

"No, sir," she responded politely. "As I said, our operations are covert. But you can always speak with General Greg Yarrow, who oversees our operations. He'll vouch for us."

"I've already done that. He's as closemouthed as you." The colonel settled back, apparently deciding that confronting her antagonistically wasn't getting him anywhere. "Okay, tell me about your initial impressions. Did you see anything that might help accomplish your mission as fast as we need it done?"

"Not yet, but I'll make sure we do our best to bring down the perpetrators as quickly as possible, sir," she said, purposely obscure.

"I'm sure you will." The colonel rose, using his bulk to move his chair from beneath his desk. She was clearly about to be dismissed—and was glad. "What's your next move?"

"I want to retrieve my therapy dog from my assistant and start my visits to the appropriate floors first. Then I'll check out the infectious diseases wing, start seeing patients soon."

"Those areas aren't where you'll find anything relating to our thefts." He snapped at her once more, and she swallowed her irritated retort.

"No, sir. But I hope to be of service as a medical doctor, as well as visiting patients with my dog. Both are part of my cover, and as a doctor dealing with infectious diseases I'll oversee extraction of the kinds of samples from patients that can become biohazards like those that were stolen. I'll report anything I find of potential interest to you."

"Yeah, you do that. Meantime, I'll get you started with your medical duties." He lifted the receiver on the phone on his desk and pushed a button. "Is he here yet?" he immediately asked whomever answered. "Good. Send him in." He looked at Grace. "One of our other infectious-disease specialists will take you to that wing and introduce you around, since I assume you didn't meet anyone there yesterday with all the paperwork you were doing."

A shudder of warning immediately passed through Grace. It was all she could do to continue just to sit and keep an impassive yet interested expression on her face.

It surely wouldn't be...

A knock sounded on the closed office door. Whoever was there opened it without waiting for the colonel's response.

An instant later, a man walked into the room. He was tall, broad-shouldered beneath a white medical jacket similar to Grace's but much larger. He was great-looking, with longish thick black hair and a sharp facial structure. His straight, dark eyebrows and wide lips underscored his angry-looking scowl as he glanced at her. The look lightened considerably as he turned to the colonel. "Good morning," he said.

"You ready to show Dr. Andreas around?" Colonel Otis asked.

"Of course." He turned back toward her. This time, his expression was neutral, but it still sent shivers cascading down Grace's spine.

It was Simon Parran. He looked even better than he had all those years ago, if that was possible. And she had indeed caught his intriguing masculine scent last night.

Chapter 2

"Hello, Grace." Simon continued to stride into the room when he saw her. Of course he had expected to see her here. Colonel Otis had ordered Simon to act as her tour guide that day.

For reasons he didn't want to think about too deeply, he had agreed without objection.

Grace rose from a chair facing the colonel's desk and turned. Her movements were slow and supple, her expression neutral. "Hi, Simon," she said in a soft, cool monotone.

"So you've met." Colonel Nelson Otis sounded irritated, as if he'd planned some startling introduction. Like, *Parran, you stupid civilian doctor, I want you to meet this pretty lady physician who was smart enough to join the military.* Otis had made it clear he held the civilians around here in disdain. "I thought you'd mostly dealt with the clerical staff yesterday, Dr. Andreas," Otis continued, "filling out forms, reviewing hospital policies and all that."

"Pretty much." Grace crossed the room toward Simon. She didn't mention that they'd met before. A good thing. Otherwise, they might have to explain the circumstances, and that could be uncomfortable even now. She held out her hand for a businesslike shake. "Good to see you again, Simon."

Her grip was firm, even as her sable-brown eyes flashed with her lie. She'd been one hell of a good-looker back then. Now, she was even more beautiful, if that was possible: slender in her scrubs and medical jacket, with pert facial features including high cheekbones. Her silver-blond hair had been longer before. Now it was styled in a shaggy cut that brushed her eyebrows and skimmed her shoulders. She smelled like flowers, light and fragrant, yet there was also something heavier about her scent. Something damned appealing. And familiar. He'd imagined smelling it again from the moment he'd heard the name Grace Andreas once more.

Her lips were pursed, but he suspected they'd still be highly enjoyable to kiss.

Not that he'd ever get the chance to test that theory.

"Good to see you, too," he said, sorry to realize that he meant it. Many of the times he'd thought of Grace during the years since they'd met in their first term of pre-med studies, he'd wondered if she had followed through, become a doctor. If so, where she practiced. If not, what else she'd done with her life.

He could have found out. The Internet was filled with resources that could tell him.

He purposely hadn't looked.

"So," he said, "you ready to go see the Charles Carder Infectious Diseases Center?"

"Sure." She turned back to the commander and saluted smartly. "Thank you, sir."

Yeah, Simon got it even before seeing her. She was in the military despite being dressed like him. The idea turned him off—a little, at least. He had joined the medical staff for reasons of his own. It didn't mean he had to like the fact that this hospital was affiliated with, and run by, the military.

What he did like was its amazingly useful lab facilities. And that he could visit them frequently, with few questions and no impediments.

He opened the door and let Grace walk briskly through the secretary's area and beyond, into the wide hallway of the admin wing. It was on the top floor, the third.

"We need to go down a floor to get to the infectious diseases center," Simon told Grace. "The stairs are there." He pointed to a closed door with a sign above depicting a stairway.

"I figured," Grace said drily.

"Would you prefer the elevator?" Simon asked.

"The stairs are fine."

That was the extent of their conversation until they were on the second floor. The silence was anything but comfortable.

As they started walking along the polished floors of the long, meandering hallway, past other hospital wings, Grace said, "So you're in internal medicine now. Interesting. I'd have figured you for emergency medicine, years ago, or maybe surgery. Better yet, an area related to anatomy. Or something else altogether, like dermatology. Or veterinary medicine." She looked up at him challengingly.

Why did that expression on her beautiful face make his insides start to burn? Or maybe it was simply the sudden closeness again of Grace, after their very long separation.

"Same goes," he retorted, intentionally making his tone grating. "Are we going to start on that same woo-woo obsession of yours all over again?" He glared right back—and was discomfited to see what appeared to be a gleam of triumph in her eyes before she looked away.

As if she finally had gotten him to admit the "truth" she had goaded him for so pointedly back in pre-med.

She couldn't really know…could she?

Even if she didn't, her being here, at such a critical time to his personal experiments, could be a huge problem. He needed to work even harder, after his only partly successful test last night.

The second-floor hallway seemed to go on forever. That should have been a bad thing, considering the chilly atmosphere between them. Even so, Grace couldn't help feeling excited that she was once again in Simon's presence.

Although it hurt. She couldn't turn off her emotions now any more than she'd been able to way back when they'd known each other.

She had loved Simon, nearly from the time they had met in their first pre-med classes at Michigan State University. Their passion had been nearly overwhelming, their lovemaking incredible and intense.

And then he was gone. He transferred to another school at the end of the first term.

Left her.

Never mind that she had been the one to break things off first. She had expected candor from the man she wanted to spend her life with. Instead, she had gotten equivocations. Lies.

Ridicule.

She had nearly revealed to him what she was in order to get him to disclose that he, too, was a shifter—assuming it was true.

Thanks to his derision, she'd never dared to mention it.

Good thing.

"Here we are," Simon finally said at a door with frosted windows. The wall beside it held large metallic letters reading Charles Carder Infectious Diseases Center. He held the door open, and Grace walked in.

The next half hour was a blur of introductions to the nursing staff and other physicians, and a tour of the facilities.

One person Grace met was Captain Moe Scoles, also a doctor, the head of the Infectious Diseases Center. He was working on a computer inside a moderate-sized office beside a nurse's station. Tall, with hair shorn nearly to his scalp, he gave Grace a rundown of the extra precautions taken here, where the illnesses were, of course, contagious—often highly so. Then he told Grace, "We're all staffed up today, but we'll assign you an office tomorrow and put you to work seeing patients."

"Thanks, sir." That meant she would have the afternoon to start something else she intended to do—all with the design of aiding in her real mission.

To get started, she needed to cut short her uncomfortable interlude with Simon. "Thanks for showing me around," she told him once they were back in the corridor.

"You're welcome." His golden-brown eyes bored into hers. "It really is good to see you again, Grace." He sounded surprised, the words apparently erupting from him without forethought. His wide lips immediately flattened as if he were trying to withdraw what he'd said.

She couldn't help smiling at his sudden unease. "I'm as surprised about it as you are." She kept her words intentionally ambiguous. "I'm sure we'll see each other around. Don't worry. I don't bite." Catching the slight widening of his eyes, she couldn't help adding, "Do you?"

She hurried down the hall—but not before hearing a burst of laughter from behind her.

Okay, she had intended to goad him, Simon thought as he started to walk in the opposite direction to look in on a patient. But it had nevertheless struck him as humorous. This time.

But the reason they'd broken up was because Grace had tried hard to get him to admit he was a shapeshifter. She hadn't been teasing about it—or so he'd believed.

She'd even hinted that she might be one too. For a while, he had hoped it was true, had interpreted her scent, her movements, as if she was. How great it would have been, if they'd had something so profound in common.

But after what his extended family had gone through before he went off to school…well, he wasn't about to burst out with the truth, trust just anyone, even someone who'd gotten under his skin that way.

She hadn't given up. Her insistence rubbed him wrong, and he'd just poked fun at her— supposedly—ridiculous claims.

And then she'd backed off. Good thing he hadn't said anything—though he still wished he knew why she'd zeroed in on him. Was she related to that murderous group? He didn't want to think so. But to protect himself and his family, *he'd* backed off too.

And in retrospect…?

Well, hell. After all this time, it didn't matter. She was in the military, so he'd been right. She couldn't be a shifter. Back then, something about him, something he'd said or done, had simply made her curious. Hopefully, now that she was older, wiser and a whole lot more distant from him, she'd lay off the subject.

Except, perhaps, to make jokes about it.

But he had to stay away from her. As far as possible, despite, or possibly because of, the way she still attracted him.

He didn't want her, or anyone else, interfering with what he was here to accomplish.

At lunchtime, Simon headed toward the stairway to the medical center's lobby floor, where the cafeteria was located beyond the auditorium. On his way, he heard children's laughter from somewhere down the second-floor hallway. Curious, he veered in that direction.

And saw Grace in the large visitors' lounge with a dog that looked mostly German shepherd. Three kids were there, too, dressed in hospital gowns. Half a dozen nurses also watched.

The dog, wearing a vest identifying it as a therapy dog, was sitting on its haunches, waving both paws in the air. That brought another peal of laughter from the children—two boys and a girl.

One boy—Sammy—was Simon's patient. He'd had such a severe case of gastroenteritis that he'd had to be hospitalized. He had tested positive for norovirus, which was highly contagious, so the kid had been pretty much isolated until well on the mend. He was due to go home tomorrow.

Simon's enhanced sense of smell had helped in his diagnosis, as always—as well as confirmation that Sammy was healing.

No problem now with him being with the other children—or being entertained by the German shepherd. It now had its head in Sammy's lap, and the boy petted it gently while the other kids watched in envy.

Simon drew closer, leaning his shoulder against the wall and crossing his arms as he watched. Grace smiled angelically as she, too, regarded the scene. She was more relaxed than she'd seemed before with him. That somehow made her look sexier, too. He tried to hold back his smile as he continued to observe.

The dog next nuzzled the little girl's hand as she sat in a metal-armed chair. The child squealed "Tilly!" in delight and leaped up toward the dog.

The dog—presumably Tilly—ran away, but when she turned back her head was down submissively, her tail wagging.

"Gently, honey." Grace took the little girl's hand, leading her to Tilly and showing her how to pet the dog.

Soon, Tilly slowly approached the remaining boy, who had apparently learned his lesson. He sat still until the dog nuzzled his hand, then stroked her head gently. When Tilly finally moved away, Grace gestured, and the dog stood up on her hind legs and danced in a circle—earning a treat.

Simon had little doubt that all three kids would heal a bit faster now, thanks to the minutes of pleasure Tilly gave them.

"Show's over, gang," Grace said. Everyone clapped—Simon included. She seemed to notice him then and aimed her smile at him.

He momentarily considered turning his grin into a scowl. Hadn't he vowed to stay away from her?

Instead, he felt his smile widen.

As the nurses collected the children, he gave a fake salute to Grace and headed down the hall.

Grace had noticed Simon the moment he appeared in the corridor. She had sucked in her breath when he had stopped to watch Tilly do her performance with the kids.

Sure, she would continue to run into him. Would even seek him out, if necessary to her mission. But the past would remain the past.

So why had she felt so breathless at the sight

of him? And so self-conscious, as if Tilly and she were both on display and needed to impress him.

She knew the answer. He was still so damned sexy that she couldn't help being constantly aware of his appealing maleness. And remembering what he was like in bed...

That was in the past too, she chided herself. It wouldn't happen again.

"Let's go, Tilly." She snapped on her dog's leash. They weren't yet through with the patient therapy she'd hoped to accomplish that day, before she took on treating patients tomorrow. For now, she was relying on Kristine to do the initial recon work—like learning all the ways to approach the biohazards storage area.

Later, Grace would commence her own recon. From Colonel Otis, she had learned the location of the laboratories where patient samples were taken for testing—samples that, if from the most harmful of communicable diseases, could be turned into potentially lethal biohazards. She would visit there later, when fewer people would be wandering the hospital's halls.

For now, Grace headed for the hospital's senior-care unit. Some colleagues who also worked with therapy dogs were much too depressed after visiting patients whose cognition was severely impaired by age-related diseases. Grace, though, found it stirring to see people whom she'd been told barely moved, or recognized anyone, perk up at seeing an energetic, caring animal like Tilly.

Grace had told the nurses ahead of time about her impending visit. Half-a-dozen seniors, mostly in wheelchairs and with blankets over their laps, sat in a semicircle in a lounge similar to that where Tilly and she had met with the children. This therapy session, too, resulted in lots of laughter, even with some patients who stared off into the distance until Tilly bumped them with her nose.

This time, no Simon observed them. Just as well. He was too much of a distraction.

For their planned final session of the day, Grace led Tilly to the psychiatric unit. As with the senior unit, it was behind a locked door to ensure no patient walked away without a doctor's approval. Having the door click shut behind them hadn't bothered Grace in the seniors' area. Here, she wasn't clear what to expect from the patients, so she felt a little uneasy.

Ten patients waited in this lounge—eight men and two women, most in cotton robes tied over their hospital gowns.

The head nurse, whose name tag read Ellie

Yong, came up to Grace. "Mostly PTSD patients," she said softly, as if conveying something confidential. But in a major military hospital like Charles Carder, that's what Grace had anticipated.

She soon lost her uneasiness—most of it, at least—during the nurses' welcome. They introduced Grace and Tilly first and then the patients, calling each by name. Some were quiet, yet stared at her mistrustfully. She assumed they were still in the deepest stages of posttraumatic stress disorder. Several were apparently undergoing detoxification for drug addiction, since she scented some of the medicines often used to help.

One patient, Sgt. Norman Ivers, seemed almost angry about having the dog around, yelling at Tilly and looming over her until the poor dog lay down submissively. Grace determined to tell the nurses to keep him in his room next time Tilly and she visited.

Another, Sgt. Jim Kubowski, seemed utterly indifferent at first, but when Tilly sat in front of him and offered her paw, he shook it, then got down on the floor and hugged the dog.

One patient, PFC George Harper, seemed to really adore Tilly. Another, Pvt. Alice Johns, knelt on the floor and cried on Tilly, and Grace vowed to bring the dog back as often as possible to cheer her.

Soon, Tilly had run through her repertoire of tricks. Their visit was over. "We'll be back soon," Grace assured those patients who appeared to give a damn.

She enjoyed this part of her assignment, working with all kinds of patients with Tilly as a therapy dog.

Too bad the rest of her mission wasn't as likely to give her this much enjoyment.

In the hallway outside the psychiatric unit, Grace considered what to do next. It was getting late, but there was still some daylight. She intended to explore parts of the hospital she hadn't seen yet, but it remained too early for what she wanted to do.

Instead, she went outside onto the hospital grounds and called Kristine on her cell phone. Her aide said she was around the side of the hospital building with Bailey.

They met up at the sidewalk near the curved patient drop-off area. Grace asked softly, "Have you found anything out yet? Do you know where the entrance to that tunnel is?"

"Of course," Kristine asserted. "That's what I do—figure out what you'll want to see and locate it."

Grace laughed. "Does that mean you've figured out who we're after so we can easily track down our suspect?"

The sergeant smiled. "Wouldn't want to take away your fun, ma'am." She gave a mock salute.

Their dogs leashed beside them, Kristine led Grace toward the emergency-room entrance at the side of the medical center's largest wing, then around the corner to a delivery area. Fortunately, nothing was going on there. She used her security card to get all four of them back inside the facility.

The tunnel entrance was off a room filled with boxes of benign medical supplies like bandages—but not far from the door to a stairway that, Grace determined, most likely led down to the floor containing labs where fluids and other samples were tested. Made sense, she thought.

Making sure no one was around to see them, they entered the tunnel. Grace saw no particular security there, but not many people were likely to know about this passageway, except staff members who delivered the biohazards to their storage area beyond the main outdoor parking lot. Grace and Kristine and the dogs walked swiftly along the concrete corridor, the sound of their footsteps echoing slightly in the confined area. It was illuminated by occasional recessed lights, and Grace's nose wrinkled at the dry, musty scent of the surrounding emptiness.

Soon they reached the end. Kristine carefully opened the door and peered out. "We're okay." She held the door open, then led Grace and the dogs through a large, nearly empty parking lot toward its far end.

"There." She pointed toward the concrete outbuilding Grace had seen briefly before—twice, including while shifted. She'd left it to Kristine to start gathering details about it.

The building was compact and nondescript, with a couple of doors visible. It could have been for storage of garden equipment, or electrical fuses and circuitry for the hospital—whatever. The fenced area around it contained yuccas and palm trees and other drought-tolerant plants that were politically correct for this dry climate. The only thing that indicated it was more than a boring, ordinary storage shed was the illuminated office at one end. In it sat a couple of uniformed soldiers.

"Have you talked to the guards?" Grace asked Kristine.

"Yep, at least the ones on duty earlier. They try to keep their presence low-key, like they're just guarding the parking lot and not what's behind that door."

"But some biohazards were stolen while guys were on watch?"

"Seems that way."

"Interesting. I'll need to find out the excuses given by whomever was on duty during the times samples were taken from here."

"Count me in," Kristine said. "Sounds like fun. The building's not as bland as it looks, by the way." She pointed toward the door farthest to the left. "On that side is the incineration unit where they dispose of the biohazards."

"Why do they do it here, I wonder?" Grace mused. "Aren't there companies that are specially rigged to pick up this kind of material to dispose of it offsite, away from the hospitals?"

"I gather it's because of the volume and security issues," Kristine said. "Better to deal with it here than take the chance someone will hijack a disposal truck."

"A bit of irony," Grace said.

"Seems that way," her aide acknowledged. "Anyway, it's nice and eco-friendly, I gather— everything's burned, not much ash, nothing escapes into the air. Poof, and the danger is gone…unless the stuff's stolen first."

"And that's exactly what we need to stop," said Grace.

Grace considered asking Kristine to take Tilly back to their quarters on the air-force base, but it was time for one further piece of exploration, and she wanted her cover dog along.

A short while later, Grace walked slowly along the dimly lit corridor deep in the bowels of the Charles Carder Medical Center. Her rubber-soled shoes made no noise on the gleaming linoleum floor, although Tilly's nails clicked lightly.

She spotted security cameras that hadn't been doing their job reliably. Neither had other security devices, including those requiring people to use key cards to enter this floor. Many tests were conducted in the multiple labs on this level of the hospital. But all that security, including locked doors and storage cabinets, and guards out by the storage area, hadn't prevented the disappearance of biohazard materials collected from patients with potentially dangerous communicable diseases. They weren't always large samples, but their theft was enough to worry those who knew.

Hence Grace's mission.

What was that? Tilly had heard the soft click, too. She had been well trained not to bark, which would scare off any subject of their hunt. Instead, she sat still on the slick floor and looked up at Grace, waiting for a command.

Grace held up her hand in the signal that meant "good girl." Then she gave the signal for Tilly to stay.

This was only her second day here. Would it be this easy for her to discover the perpetrator of the thefts? That would be ideal for the U.S. government, and even for Alpha Force.

But Grace had hoped to utilize her very special shifting powers more to fulfill her mission…

Her back against the wall, she slid along the hall toward where the click had originated—the opening of one of the many doors along this corridor?

Yes—one only a few feet away from her swung inward. Grace reached down toward her weapon, a small revolver she'd retrieved from Kristine before heading down here this night and hid in a holster strapped to her waist beneath her loose white medical jacket. As a doctor in addition to her other assets and skills, she believed in preserving life—except at the expense of another's…or hers.

She hadn't really expected to need to use the gun, but she was prepared, just in case.

In another instant, a man opened a door and strode into the hall.

It was Simon.

Chapter 3

"What are you doing here, Grace?" Simon demanded, knowing he sounded defensive. Was she following him?

If so, how? As always, he'd checked around the area carefully before going into the lab. Listened. Scented the air. No one had been around.

He'd have known, especially if it was Grace—wouldn't he?

But he was imagining her everywhere now. He'd already acknowledged to himself that the tour he'd given her had been far from the first time he thought he sensed her after learning she'd be around.

Even early yesterday, when he shifted back

to human form at daybreak, he had thought—worried—that she was nearby. Had even believed he caught her addictive scent.

He was often hazy, though, during and immediately after a shift, especially an uncontrolled one at the full moon. And now, even a partially controlled one. That was something he intended to fix by perfecting what he had just been working on in the lab behind him.

His formulation would not, however, help his imagination.

Grace had motioned for her dog to sit on the hallway floor beside her. Now she regarded Simon coolly yet with a hint of amusement. As if she recalled the old days, when he'd made such an effort to answer each of her questions with another question. Or to otherwise turn the discussion around against her.

It hadn't worked well then. It wouldn't work now.

"Tilly and I have been on a walk, exploring our new environment," she finally responded. "And you, Simon? What brings you to this floor so late at night?" She peered around his shoulder toward the door from which he had emerged, now closed behind him.

He didn't want her going in there and snooping—or even reporting his presence to anyone else. Of course he still had his stock, planned answers if—and, most likely, when—he was questioned about being here at this hour. He was simply too busy during the daytime to mix the homeopathic healing formulations he was working on to help his patients. When he had applied for the job at Charles Carder more than a year ago, he'd brought samples of some energy tablets and nutritional supplements he'd been working on to help recuperating infectious-disease patients regain their strength. Testimonials, too, from physicians and nurse practitioners and others who had used them. Harmless stuff that wouldn't require any government approvals.

Genuine? Sure. But also a good cover for what he really was working on.

Though authorized to be present, he had carefully selected a lab outside the area surveyed by security cameras. Not that he would do anything obvious outside the lab that shouldn't be caught on camera.

He had an ulterior motive for being at this location, sure. But he wouldn't admit it to Grace. He had a feeling she had an ulterior motive, too—and was just as unlikely to spill it to him.

"Not over that old curiosity of yours, are you, Grace?" He attempted to sound amused.

"Don't worry about me. I'm approved to be here." Partly. "I'm conducting officially sanctioned business that I can't get to during the day. But you? Since you're in the military and probably got briefed about this place, you may already have heard about some local thefts recently. For the safety of this hospital and its personnel, I've got the right to ask questions of people who may not be authorized to be in this area, and to report to those in charge. So tell me, what are you *really* doing here?"

Her lovely brown eyes had widened slightly before her demeanor grew bland once more. "Interesting. May I ask whom you report to about unauthorized visitors?"

She hadn't answered his question—again. "No," he responded to hers, "you may not." Mostly because he'd lied. He reported, in this as in the rest of his life, only to himself—as much as he could get away with.

He had gathered, from her brief change of expression, that she was at least familiar with the thefts. Involved? Maybe. That would explain her questioning his presence. He'd keep an eye on her, just in case.

At least that gave him a good excuse. He only hoped he wouldn't come to regret her presence any more than he already did.

* * *

Grace wanted to scream. To kick Simon right in his smug, gorgeous face—or somewhere else he'd notice.

He'd dared to remind her of the old days, even as he was baiting her all over again. Not answering her questions. Asking his own.

And still managing to get her hormones all stirred into a cauldron of seething, sexually arousing juices.

"Have a good night, Simon," she finally said, signaling to Tilly to stand. They started briskly down the hall.

Grace wondered immediately if Simon would spend this night, or any others, alone. Someone as hot as he undoubtedly had a significant other waiting for him, panting, in bed. Maybe not a wife—she'd checked, and he wasn't wearing a wedding ring. But a lot of married physicians didn't wear rings because it was hard to keep them sanitized, or to avoid catching them in sensitive equipment.

Did she believe anything he said? Oh, she felt certain he had rigged some arguably legitimate reason to be in this area, even at night. But could she trust that he was keeping an eye out for whoever was stealing the biohazard samples, rather than doing it himself?

She would keep close watch on him. It was part of her mission.

She'd love every minute—especially if she could prove that Simon was the thief she was after.

Early the next morning, all four Alpha Force members, plus two dogs, gathered upstairs in the furnished quarters assigned to Grace.

As they all took seats in her compact living room, Grace asked Lt. Autumn Katers, a recent recruit, "How's your alter ego?" Like Grace, Autumn always brought her cover animal along on missions—a female red-tailed hawk who was initially trained for falconry.

"Venus is fine. Wonderful, in fact." Autumn settled into her seat on the bland umber sofa.

"We'll take her out for some fresh air once we're done talking," said Sgt. Ruby Belmont, who had opted for one of two stiff wooden chairs dragged in from the small kitchen. "We'll give her as much flying time as she wants." A tall, thin woman with glasses, Ruby was Autumn's aide on Alpha Force missions. Like all shapeshifters' backups, she helped take care of the cover animals—and watched their shifters' backs while they, too, were in animal form.

Grace was continually pleased by how well

her aide, Kristine, accomplished her job, and believed Ruby and she got along well. Right now, Kristine sat on the other kitchen chair, and Bailey lay on the floor next to Tilly.

"Okay, are we ready to report in?" Grace had selected the rust-colored armchair at the end of the coffee table so she could be more or less in the middle of the gang.

"Go for it," said Autumn.

Using a special high-tech phone she'd brought on the mission for just this purpose, Grace pressed in the number for their commanding officer, Major Drew Connell, who expected their call.

"About time you reported in," came his voice immediately after the first ring. He was in a time zone three hours later than theirs, so it would be 0930 at Ft. Lukman. Grace knew, though, that he referred not to the time today, but that they had been around a couple of days already.

"Ah, but I'm sure you loved the suspense of waiting," she said lightly. "Only—well, nothing much to report so far, sir." She gave a rundown of her first couple of days at the medical center, followed by her late walk-through last night with Tilly. "The lab floor, where biohazard materials are taken to be tested, was pretty quiet. I only saw one person—a doctor. He seemed reluctant to talk about why he was there, so I'll find out more about him, but he's my only potential suspect so far." Grace didn't mention she had a personal history with that doctor, although she suspected it would eventually have to be revealed.

Next, Autumn gave her report. Her cover as a communications officer allowed her to access the base's aircraft hangars. She hadn't been around long enough to explore them all, but she'd seen nothing suspicious in those she'd visited so far.

Ruby, too, had a background in aviation, so she had also started checking out the base's facilities, but hadn't yet done anything worth mentioning, other than fiddling with some of the security cameras on the night of the full moon.

Kristine finished. "Bailey and I walked the hospital grounds several times, especially near the remote storage area at the far end of one of the parking lots, and I showed Grace the tunnel leading to it—a way the test materials are transported. I've talked to a few military guards who hang out in that area, and I assume some materials are being stored there now. Nothing notable about the building housing the incinerator, either."

"Good job, all of you," Drew Connell said.

"Now, get busy. We need results as quickly as possible."

"How's Melanie?" Grace asked. Drew's wife, Dr. Melanie Harding-Connell, a veterinarian, had introduced Grace to Alpha Force. She was pregnant with the couple's first baby. She wasn't a shifter, but Drew was.

"Getting along fine," Drew said. "She's due within the next few weeks."

"Our best to all of you," Grace said, and hung up. She'd be interested in learning all about the baby's arrival in this sort-of mixed marriage.

A short while later, Grace walked with Kristine to the medical center. They'd left both dogs in Grace's apartment to keep each other company, since there would be no therapy visits today. Neither would Kristine snoop about the hospital grounds. They'd both just perform the jobs that were their covers, as would Autumn and Ruby.

Grace was glad that this assignment made use of her background as a doctor. Alpha Force was, not surprisingly, a small unit, and its members handled whatever missions they were assigned. She knew that recently Lt. Patrick Worley, also a physician, had played the role of a dog musher in Alaska to apprehend some pretty nasty bad guys.

Once at the hospital, Grace went to the doctors' lounge, where she again donned a clean white medical jacket over her scrubs and pinned on her name tag. Then she started her rounds, saying hello to the nurses at their stations and visiting rooms of patients she'd already been assigned.

And watching for other doctors…but no sign of Simon this morning. At least not yet. Would he try to avoid her?

That wasn't like the Simon she'd known— until he'd transferred to another school.

The first patient Grace saw was a woman whose child had brought home Fifth disease from school—a common illness causing a facial rash. By the time the redness appeared, the illness was no longer contagious, but it was easy to pass to others before symptoms were obvious. It was mostly harmless. However, this particular mother had suffered severe anemia as a result and had been hospitalized. Fortunately she was doing well, and Grace didn't spend much time with her.

When she went back into the hall, a nurse hurried over. "Dr. Andreas, the E.R. called and requested that all infectious disease specialists head there. Only two of you are on duty right now. Several patients were brought in with something that might be contagious and they need a fast diagnosis."

Grace hurried down the stairs to the E.R. There, she asked the nurse in charge about the situation for which she had been summoned and was directed to an area down the main hallway. When she walked into the large preliminary examination room, she noted several nurses including Kristine, six apparent patients, and Simon, who stalked out of one of the patient cubicles separated from each other by long blue curtains. He wore gloves and a sanitary mask covering the lower part of his face, but there was no mistaking his muscular build and dark hair.

Grace quickly donned a mask and gloves, too, then approached as he removed his gloves and scrubbed his hands at the large sink. "What does it look like, doctor?"

Simon stepped back. Grace was struck by the intensity and concern in his golden-brown eyes. "Symptoms include diarrhea, vomiting, fever and severe abdominal cramps. The six who just came in are a flight instructor at the base, his family and a couple of neighbors, who ate take-out food from a restaurant a few miles from this area last night. Chicken salad, they said. My suspicion is shigellosis, since that restaurant had problems with it a while back—sanitary conditions suspect, cited by the local board of health. Could be something else, though. Their symptoms seem a lot more severe than what we saw before. We'll need tests run."

"Life-threatening?" Grace asked tersely. At Simon's nod, she hurried into the first examining station.

The next half hour was busy—especially because several other patients with similar symptoms were brought in. Whether it was a severe dysentery-like outbreak of the highly infectious shigellosis or something different—something worse—it appeared to have resulted from food from the same dining facility. Grace directed that lab techs obtain fecal and other samples from each patient and take them to be tested. She assumed that Simon did the same.

The smells in the ER area were nauseating, especially, Grace assumed, because of her enhanced senses even while in human form. But as a doctor, she had encountered odors as bad, or even worse, before. After examining each patient and directing the medical tests to be taken, Grace moved on to the next. Simon appeared equally busy.

Eventually, a lab tech returned with a preliminary result. Simon had apparently been correct: shigellosis, but a highly toxic strain, perhaps a mutated bacterial version. Almost all the patients appeared ill enough to be admitted to the medical facility. Grace prescribed antibiotics—hoping that this strain was not resistant—as well as other medications to ease the severe symptoms.

After a while, the worst of the emergency seemed over, although a couple of patients remained in serious condition. Grace's adrenaline was still pumping, but she felt she'd done well in helping the majority of the admittees. She'd keep a close watch on those who were the most ill.

She'd also been highly impressed while observing Simon in action. He might be sharp-tongued and enigmatic when dealing with her, but she truly admired his gentle, caring attitude while dealing with suffering patients.

What a conglomeration of contrasts this man still appeared to be. Was he a viable suspect in the biohazards thefts?

She peeled off her latest pair of gloves as well as the mask, and headed again toward the room's main sink. Unsurprisingly, Simon was there, too.

"What a morning!" she exclaimed. "It'll

be interesting to get a case history on each of them. Confirm that the infection came from the restaurant, although that seems pretty clear."

"Right." He didn't look at her as he dried his hands on a paper towel from a sanitary container.

"We'll have to keep a close watch still, of course, to make sure that the antibiotics we prescribed are effective. And—"

"You're right, Grace. As always. See you later." He turned his back and started walking away.

Obviously he had no interest in talking to her just then. Well, so what? She was busy, too.

Still, she felt inordinately hurt by his slight. She had an urge to kick him in that nice, firm butt she watched with angry interest as he headed for the examination-room's door.

And followed him. As she exited the room after him, she called, "Yeah, see you later, Dr. Parran," and headed in the opposite direction. Feeling upset. Angry.

Not a good time for her cell phone to ring. Especially when it was her commanding officer, Major Drew Connell.

She walked out a door for privacy as she answered.

"Any new developments, Grace? I heard

from Colonel Otis that they're likely to have a large enough batch of contaminants to incinerate them tonight or tomorrow."

"I wondered about that," Grace said. "Especially after today." Holding the phone tight against her ear in the warm breeze as she strolled along a path beside the building, she related what had occurred in the emergency room that morning. "A lot of samples of probable shigellosis-infected fluids were collected, maybe a more virulent strain than we normally see. We still have work to ensure the outbreak is stopped. Plus, we have to make sure no one gets hold of these samples and creates a man-made shigellosis outbreak. I know some strains are fairly harmless, and the disease can't be passed to more than a few people at a time, but it sometimes appears on lists of possible biological weapons, since the worst varieties can get pretty severe and there's no vaccine."

"So you and Kristine, and maybe Autumn and Ruby, too—how about keeping watch on that supposedly secret storage area in the parking lot tonight? This might be when our bad guys make their move. And it might be a good thing to have different perspectives in addition to human."

"That's what I thought, too. I'll take a look

around, and if it appears useful I'll shift. I'll also tell Autumn to. We'll report to you in the morning."

For the rest of the day, Simon avoided Grace as much as possible.

Too many possibilities of her getting in his way. Asking questions.

Distracting him with her luscious body as well as her inevitable curiosity.

He regretted—to some extent—his abruptness with her, but he needed to step back. Get some perspective. Ensure that he had time, and his thoughts, to himself that night.

He hadn't been joking with Grace last night, near his lab. Biohazard materials had been stolen before around here—including during the prior outbreak of shigellosis, which seemed a lot more benign than this one.

The latest shigella bacterial samples would be a practical haul for the thief.

"What do you think?" Grace asked Kristine. They were in Grace's car in the parking lot behind the medical center. Both were in civilian T-shirts and jeans, to blend in with visitors to the medical center once they exited the vehicle. They'd left their dogs in their living quarters again, at least for now.

"The best places for a wolf to hide aren't too near this building." Her aide peered first at the open space near the building, then away from the rows of cars and toward the vegetated areas near the perimeter fencing.

"My thoughts, too. A hawk, though—maybe only Autumn should shift tonight and just perch somewhere to watch."

"Sounds good. I'll let Autumn and Ruby know."

He prowled. At the edges of the medical center.

Hiding in bushes. Sometimes between cars. Concern about being seen. But he was faster, now, than any human. More cunning.

Elation. His shift, late this night, was on his own terms. His human awareness, in wolf form, was the best ever.

He would watch where samples were stored. He would—

Wait. The sounds. Human voices in distress, and more.

The smells—ugly. Unnatural here.

Something was wrong.

He carefully slunk toward the area, staying in shadows.

All night so far, Grace had felt frustrated. She'd hoped to shift into wolf form, but she knew her decision and Kristine's made sense.

Instead, only Autumn shifted, as they'd discussed. The others had, one by one, pulled their cars into the area near the outbuilding and parked, looking as if they were there to visit a patient in the medical center. Each walked casually by the glassed-in office where the guards sat and peeked in. Then they drove somewhere else and parked again, and covertly kept an eye on the area.

Kristine had gone first. Then Ruby. Then Grace, and then they started the routine all over again. They all reported to one another by phone.

"I saw a little activity in the office," Ruby had said a few minutes ago, after her second swing through the parking lot. "Could be a delivery was made then, since a couple of people were there in hospital jackets. I hid behind a van and watched for a while. They left and the guards settled back down. Everything appeared fine."

Now it was Grace's second turn. She pulled once more into the parking lot and drove toward the far end. She parked several rows from the building, finding a spot near a couple of other cars in the sparsely occupied lot. Then she sauntered in the direction of the building, surrounded by its drought-tolerant landscaping.

Was that the scent of a wolf? A shifter? Or was her mind playing tricks?

She looked around, peering into shadows, seeing and hearing no movement. But the scent did not go away.

Was she simply daydreaming of Simon… again?

She tried to shrug off the sensations as she neared the guards' office. She saw no one through the glass window.

Could they be on a break? Unlikely that they'd both be gone at the same time.

Grace looked around. She still saw no one else around. And then she inhaled deeply, purposely invoking her enhanced senses once more.

That's when she smelled a different scent—something incongruously chemical in the warm night air.

"Damn!" she whispered as she put her hand over her pocket, feeling the small pistol she had hidden there, just in case. She headed toward the guard enclosure.

The scent, though still faint, grew stronger the closer she got.

The gate in the wire fence wasn't locked, and Grace burst through it. By the time she looked through the window into the building, she suspected what she would see: two bodies in uniform, lying on the floor. Were they still alive?

She pulled out her weapon, sighting along it as she pivoted. She saw no one else. Leaving the door open to dissipate any remaining chemical in the air so she could enter as safely as possible, she hurried in, felt for pulses. Yes, thank heavens. They were merely unconscious.

One more thing to do, then, before calling for assistance. She checked the door to the adjoining storage area.

It was unlocked. No surprise.

Neither was she surprised to see that it was empty.

The biohazards specimens were gone.

Chapter 4

"You're sure you want to do this now?" Kristine asked.

Grace stood with her aide in almost total darkness, sheltered by hedges, between the hospital grounds and air-force base. Nighttime heat surrounded them, as well as the slight aroma of jet fuel. They had left both dogs in their apartments.

The investigation of the theft was currently the focus of the security units at both the hospital and the air-force base, but no one was scouring this remote location—not for this moment, at least.

"There's no better time," Grace said.

"But there's too much activity. You'll be seen."

"I'll be careful. If I get in trouble, you can create a diversion."

"Yeah," Kristine grumbled. "And then I can get arrested for being the thief."

"You're too good for that." Grace gave Kristine a joking punch on the arm. "Besides, you brought Tilly's leash and collar, didn't you?" She looked at the large backpack that Kristine wore over her camo-colored T-shirt and khaki shorts. Except for the backpack, the outfit matched Grace's.

"Of course."

"Then if I'm seen, you'll—"

"Tell everyone that your dog escaped from your quarters and I'm looking for her, which is why I'm carrying the leash—to hook her up when I find her. As long as she remembers her manners and doesn't bark inside the apartment, that works fine."

"She's a great dog." But Grace didn't need to remind Kristine of that. They'd both worked with Tilly and with Kristine's dog, Bailey, knew they were well trained. "Okay, it's time now. I have to act fast to get access to any remaining scents or other clues before they disappear—or are hauled off as evidence."

"Yes, ma'am." Kristine gave a joking salute.

When they'd found the guards unconscious and the biohazards missing, Grace had immediately directed Kristine to call the security assigned to the hospital and tell them to send EMTs. The men's lives could be at stake.

Then they had contacted Ruby Belmont to let her know what had happened. "Is Autumn still shifted?" Grace had asked, standing outside the room containing the unconscious men. "Do you know if she saw anything?" But Autumn hadn't yet returned.

While they waited for official help to arrive, Grace had tried to use her heightened human senses to detect the scents of who had done this, but the chemical smell of whatever had been used to knock out the guards, though light, nevertheless overwhelmed any other aroma. Plus, while she was unshifted, Grace's abilities were limited.

Grace and Kristine had waited long enough to be questioned briefly by those conducting the investigation about why they happened to be in the area at that late hour. Colonel Otis had been called, and he would know their real reason, but they told the guards only that they had been taking a long walk for exercise before going to bed and had heard a groan.

Fortunately, the men stationed in the building were expected to survive, but they would probably have headaches for days, thanks to the gas used to render them unconscious. From what Grace had learned, the guards in the earliest thefts had believed they had just fallen asleep. They, too, awoke with headaches. Any chemical, and its odor, had dissipated quickly, and no source remained. Even so, its presence was suspected, but the men didn't even remember smelling anything. Later guards were told to stay alert for anything unusual, but somehow these guys were knocked out anyway.

By something that only someone like Grace, and her acute senses, was aware of.

Now Grace intended to shift as quickly as possible. She would need to remain on the periphery of the investigation, but she might be able to pick up on more evidence that the security team would never imagine was there.

Even though their current location was remote and camouflaged by tall hedges, Grace directed Kristine to an area with similar characteristics even farther from where people milled around. That's when she had Kristine take off the backpack. Grace removed the battery-operated light from it. Its beam had the intensity of the full moon when turned on.

Next, she carefully took out the special Alpha Force elixir and measured a dose for herself. It was the amazing concoction that allowed shapeshifters to change whenever they wanted, not just under a full moon.

"You ready?" Kristine asked.

"In a sec." Grace glanced around out of habit, despite having seen no other beings, human or otherwise, when she chose this secluded site between the two facilities. Then she removed her clothes. "Now," she said.

Kristine turned on the light and aimed it at her. In moments, Grace felt the usual discomfort as she started to shift.

Caution.

Despite having a plan for if she was spotted while shifted, her intent was to stay far from curious eyes.

The substantial plantings here, watered by the military for privacy and security, were useful. On the soft pads of her canine feet, she crept on the sandy dirt from behind one hedge to the next, moving from the air-force base and onto the hospital property. Drawing closer to the building that was her target.

Slowly. Listening for human voices and their locations.

Pointing her nose into the air to scent for anything, anyone, she needed to avoid.

There was less cover as she approached. Yuccas and palm trees provided little shelter.

Cars in the parking lot provided more, but they also obscured the people she needed to avoid. And maybe those she wanted to see.

She finally reached a place where she could watch the building. People in uniform still surrounded it despite the late hour. Could she wait them out?

Sentries would likely remain there for this night—more protection for this area, but too late to prevent the theft.

She would therefore prowl the periphery. Watching, listening, scenting the air and environs, just in case the thieves returned—an unlikely event.

She crouched and crept from behind one car to the next. And then another.

Then—

Her nose suddenly pointed straight up as she inhaled the scent that had just assailed her.

Another wolf? The same one she had sensed on the night of the full moon? The fur on her back bristled.

Wild Mexican wolves could be found in Arizona—a fact that helped this Alpha Force mis-

sion. More than one could be hanging out in this area. Maybe even a pack.

Or not.

She crept forward slowly, all enhanced senses on alert.

There. At the outer row of parked vehicles, she spotted movement near the ground. A flash of silver fur between cars.

Had she been noticed by her apparent counterpart? Perhaps, for suddenly he was running. Beyond the cars, past the parking lot, through stands of cacti and other plants, toward a different portion of the air-force base.

She was gaining no useful information here. The motion of the other wolf could call attention to her.

Slowly, as if stalking the other creature, she followed, heedful that the humans behind her might not be kind to either animal if spotted here.

Her quarry, too, might attack if she got close enough.

Nearer to him, the scent was different. Wilder. One she recognized as dual and heated and agitated.

The smell of a shifter during a change.

She drew closer, even more cautious.

She saw him then. Partly obscured by a row

of bushes, he thrashed wildly. A wolf, yet not a wolf, as he shifted from canine to human form.

The human form she had known she would see.

In a minute, it had ended.

Where the wolf had been stood Dr. Simon Parran.

Damn! Simon scowled into the hot darkness.

If he had remained in wolf form, he might have howled in rage and frustration. But that was the point. He had wanted to remain shifted longer, but the medication he had created to allow shifting anytime was as flawed in that respect as it was in keeping him from changing during a full moon.

What had he scented before? *Who* had he scented? He had thought he had caught the odor of another wolf. Even seen traces in the distance of a canine form.

If so, it had to be a true wolf. He could shift somewhat at will, thanks to the chemical formula he tested only on himself. Other shapeshifters would only change during a full moon.

At least as far as he knew. Those of his kind, and other shifters, avoided forming communities except for families and small packs, even then assimilating into the usual human populations. They rarely sought out others even in these days of high-tech communication. Maybe especially so, thanks to the dangers of hacking and identity exposure. It was safer that way.

He therefore didn't know what skills or advantages others like him might have developed.

Now, he hid behind a remote building on the hospital property until able to don his clothing. The only good thing this time was that he had been able to flee to the area where he had first shifted, where he had left his things.

He finished pulling on his jeans, then slipped a black T-shirt over his head. He checked his pants pocket. The small bottle where he kept his pills was still there—empty now, since he only brought the dosage needed each time he shifted in case someone found his paraphernalia. An empty pill bottle would generate fewer questions than one with a tablet that someone could try to analyze.

Taking a few deep breaths, he let his mind evaluate his body. Except for his usual slight haziness, everything had returned to human normalcy. The physical discomfort he felt while shifting had ended.

He was back.

He was also shouting inside with even greater frustration as he began walking slowly along a path toward the front of the hospital, far from where security forces now concentrated their investigation.

He had decided to shift once he'd heard the news broadcast on the hospital security system—a radio transmission he hacked into for his own purposes. Biohazard wastes had been stolen...again. The guards had been taken down first but had not been killed.

Since the official security staff had been so ineffectual, Simon had jumped in to look for information to pass along to authorities. It was a good rehearsal for using his shifting pill.

More important, it was a good attempt to use his special resources to potentially help save lives, even prevent a catastrophe. What if the thieves used the hazardous waste to create biological weapons that could sicken, and kill, an incalculable number of people? The missing samples, if cultured and expanded, might be capable of being turned into something quite dangerous.

The only people likely to steal biohazards besides terrorists were those hoping to sell the materials for some horrendous purposes—or to extort the government, demanding money for their return.

This time, he had not succeeded in stopping the incident, or even observing it in progress. If there was a next time, he would be better prepared—although maybe it was already too late.

As he walked along the side of the parking lot, his gaze drifted to the air-force base next door and the hedge-covered fence separating the two facilities.

He had heard that Grace and her aide, a nurse, had discovered the guards down and the biohazards missing. A logical assumption would be that they had stolen the stuff. They were there at the operative time. But Simon hated even to think something like that about Grace.

He snorted aloud at his stupid, gullible attitude. Was the fact she was as beautiful as ever the reason he couldn't imagine she had any evil inside her?

He hadn't trusted her years ago. Why start now?

He stopped outside the front door to the hospital, ignoring the people standing on the steps talking on cell phones. He inhaled the sweet scent wafting outside after the cleaning staff had passed through the lobby, masking the usual ugly hospital stenches of chemicals and sickness.

He had smelled and possibly seen that wolf earlier, while shifted. Grace had, long ago, hinted that she could be a shapeshifter, but he had assumed that was only because she was teasing him. Pretending to be like the jerks who had harmed his family, once he had told her a watered-down version of the tale—one in which no one had, of course, been a woo-woo character.

But what if Grace hadn't been pretending back then?

It seemed way out of whack, a coincidence of tremendous proportions, for the first wolf he had sensed around here to appear not long after she arrived. And also to be hanging out where the thefts had occurred—substances Grace was well aware of as an infectious-disease specialist.

Could he believe it? Should he believe it?

She hadn't been around for the earlier thefts. But that didn't mean she wasn't colluding with someone who was.

Maybe he had better spend a little more time around Grace to find out if she was involved. While protecting his own interests. Being with the woman he had been in lust with all those years ago might not be smart.

But, if he was careful, it just might be fun.

"Did you learn anything helpful?" Kristine asked as she handed Grace her clothes.

They were still outside, behind some hedges,

since there was always a risk going inside a building that they would run into someone.

Grace slipped her panties and bra on quickly, then reached for her T-shirt. She would have to watch what she said, even to her trusted aide.

"I'm still digesting what happened," she responded. "So far, I've found no answers."

Which was true. She had no answers about the stolen biohazards—or anything else, at least not yet. Even with her ability to retain human cognition while shifted, thanks to the special Alpha Force elixir, she needed time to think, with her full-sized human brain, while deciding what to do with her newly confirmed knowledge about Dr. Simon Parran.

How had he shifted without a full moon?

When had he shifted—after the gassing and thefts had occurred? Could he have had anything to do with that, or had he, like her, wanted to use his enhanced wolfen senses to look for the thieves and any evidence they might have left behind?

She had gotten an eyeful, even from a distance, of the wonderful, hard body she remembered. If anything, he had gotten better with age. Sexier.

Too bad she wouldn't be able to indulge in her renewed desire for him. The complications would be even vaster than simply knowing what he was—and, if she determined it was useful, confronting him with her knowledge.

Grace donned the sandals Kristine handed to her, and they started walking back toward their quarters.

"I assume you'll call Major Connell about what happened. He'll need to know, especially since I'm guessing that Colonel Otis will get in touch with him to complain."

"Gleefully so, I'd imagine," Grace said. "Though he's frustrated about the thefts and wants them to stop, he didn't seem pleased that Alpha Force was designated to help out—a group so covert that he wasn't told what its special strengths are. Yes, I'll call the major. I'd like you with me."

"Sure."

Despite the time—very early in the morning—a couple of air-force pilots whom Grace had recently met were exiting their building when Kristine and she arrived. Kristine turned slightly to watch as the two men hurried away from the building.

"Are you watching their backs or their butts?" Grace asked wryly.

"A little of both. A good Alpha Force aide needs a little distraction now and then, especially after an incident like that theft today."

"You're right." Grace preceded Kristine

inside and up the steps to her quarters. "Go get Bailey. We'll take Tilly and him for a walk before we wake up the captain. He'll understand."

Grace looked around as she headed into her apartment. Nobody around, so with luck no one would know that Tilly had been here all night—in case a strange dog that resembled her had been sighted wandering around.

As soon as Kristine arrived with Bailey, Grace called Ruby, putting her smart phone in speaker mode. "Yes," the sergeant said. "Autumn's right here."

"Did you see anything helpful?" Grace demanded when Autumn got on the phone.

"No, damn it. The guards had pizza delivered, and when the delivery guy left with a larger container than he'd gone in with, I followed. There was enough traffic that I had a hard time keeping an eye on the right car while flying at a discreet distance. When he stopped and parked at the pizza joint, I landed in a tree and watched. He removed the suspicious package from the car, all right—and pulled a few six-packs of beer out of it. And if you're going to ask me why he was receiving, and not delivering, beer, don't bother. I have no idea."

A dead end. But Grace understood why Autumn hadn't stayed to watch the building.

The shapeshifted hawk could have believed, with her human perception, that she was witnessing exactly what she had been sent to observe.

"I'm really sorry," Autumn continued. "I know I blew it, but—"

"But you could have saved the day, if things had been as they appeared to you. Don't sweat it."

Grace cut the connection and told Kristine it was time to take the dogs for their walk.

"What a fiasco," Kristine said.

"Wait till Drew Connell hears," Grace agreed.

Fifteen minutes later, they returned to Grace's unit. It was nearly 0400, a decent hour to call the major in Maryland. Grace was tired but still buzzing on adrenaline. As before, Kristine and she sat in the small living room while they called on her high-tech satellite phone, the dogs at their feet.

Major Connell answered the phone immediately. "You're up early."

"Never went to bed, sir." Grace filled him in on last night's events.

"So, even shifted, you didn't get any answers?" He didn't sound pleased. "Neither Autumn nor you."

"No, sir. Not yet, at least. But we will."

"You do that. But be careful. I'm not as concerned about someone seeing a hawk flying around, but were there any problems with your cover?"

"Not so far. I'm just like any other infectious-disease specialist at the hospital, and Sgt. Norwood is a wonderful nurse and aide."

"And last night—any possibility you were seen while shifted?"

"I don't think so, but we were prepared to have Kristine claim she was looking for Tilly." Grace reached down and patted her dog. "As if my good girl would run away like that."

"All right. I'll expect to hear from Colonel Otis later, but I'll be prepared. I trust he's been your only contact so far on security matters."

"That's right," Grace said, "though I'm considering meeting soon with Major Louis Dryson of Air Force Security Forces, in charge of security at the air-force base. Despite bringing in Alpha Force, Colonel Otis is insisting that they step up their involvement even more, too. I heard that from some of the investigators, and I'd like his take on what happened."

"As long as you stay discreet, that's fine, Grace. If you do talk to him, be sure to report how it goes. Anything else noteworthy I need to know?"

The sight of Simon changing from wolf form back to human flashed into Grace's mind—literally, as she recalled his gorgeous masculine form. But she still needed time to consider what to do about her new knowledge. She was much too tired to figure it out just then.

"No, sir," she said.

Chapter 5

Fortunately, Grace was not scheduled to report for duty at the hospital until early afternoon, and neither was Kristine. That gave them both time to catch some sleep.

Grace wondered about Simon's schedule. When would she next bump into him? How would she play it—confront him, pretend she didn't know what he was, or something in between?

She supposed she would just wing it, unless something brilliant came to her in the meantime.

She fell asleep immediately. When she woke, Tilly was pawing at the bedclothes beside her.

It was close to 1030 hours. The sweet dog undoubtedly needed to go for a walk.

Grace quickly dressed in the clothes she had worn the night before, grabbed the key to her unit and her personal cell phone, and went outside with Tilly on a leash. They walked along a paved path in the residential area, between cacti, heading away from the runways.

While Tilly sniffed the sandy dirt and decided where to accomplish her morning goals, Grace called Autumn. "Any more insight about last night?" she asked quietly, though there was no one else visible in the area.

"Nothing certain. I've been thinking about it all night. Except for that delivery fiasco, I didn't see any indication of someone fleeing the scene of a crime, even on my way back. Not that everyone stuck to the speed limits on the nearby roads or interstate, you understand. But pretty much everyone stayed with the flow of traffic. How about you? See anything interesting?"

Yes, Grace's mind responded, her thoughts again latching onto Simon. To Autumn she just said, "Nothing helpful in figuring out the theft, or who did it. But stay tuned. I let Major Connell know already, and the four of us here need to work out a new plan. This can't happen again. Not on our watch."

"Got it. You playing doctor today?"

"Yes, this afternoon."

"Talk to you later, then."

By that time, Tilly was ready to go back inside. Grace had over an hour before she needed to report to the hospital. She decided to spend some of it on the Internet, to see what the media had glommed on to about last night's incident.

She returned to her unit and booted up her computer—and was pleasantly surprised to find nothing at all about a theft at Charles Carder Medical Center last night.

Even if security was faulty and something as potentially devastating as the theft of bio-hazardous materials had occurred, at least the public wouldn't learn of it...yet.

Grace hoped that they would never need to.

"Captain Scoles would like to see you," said a nurse on duty when Grace finally reported for her shift that afternoon.

"Thanks, Jen." Grace headed for the office of the chief physician at the infectious-diseases center.

Moe Scoles was not alone. Simon Parran sat across from his desk in the compact room. Both men stood when Grace tapped on the door and walked in.

She took a deep breath. Simon's expression was neutral. Remote. As if they had never shared anything in their lives.

Probably a good thing. He would surely show some emotion if he'd any idea what she had seen last night—unless he was one damned good actor. Which could be the case.

"You wanted to see me, sir?" Grace addressed Moe.

"Please sit down, Grace." Moe pointed to a chair beside Simon.

Both men retook their seats, too. Grace didn't look at Simon again. She didn't have to. She was so aware of his presence that she felt almost as naked as she had seen him last night.

"First, I'm assigning you to an office in this wing." Moe described where it was—a small one not far from this one. Then he said, "We were just talking about the theft. I understand from one of the hospital security people that you and Sgt. Norwood were the ones who discovered it."

"I just wish we'd taken our walk earlier," she replied. "Maybe we'd have caught the thieves in the act."

Moe ran his hand over his stubble of hair. "This has to stop. Maybe it's already too late. You might not know it, but this wasn't the first time that some of the biological wastes set to be incinerated have been stolen. Much of it has been pretty nasty stuff, but those shigella bacterial samples—well, the disease has some benign forms, but this didn't seem to be one of them. Shigellosis isn't as transmittable as some of the worst diseases, but since there's no vaccine against it this could be the worst theft from here so far."

"I understand, sir," Grace said. "If there's anything different that you think we should be doing as we collect samples, or afterward, please let me know." She looked toward Simon, as if seeking his agreement. He gave a brief nod under her gaze.

"We've notified the Centers for Disease Control, but they're leaving it up to us, at least for now," Moe said.

That could be because Alpha Force had been called in on behalf of the federal government, Grace imagined, although Moe Scoles might not know that.

"We need to come up with a plan," he continued. That sounded familiar. Major Drew Connell had said so, too. The plans might be coordinated, but since Alpha Force and its mission here remained secret, Grace could not tell Moe that either. She could only discuss it with Colonel Otis—and even that had limits.

"Do you have any ideas?" She included Simon in her question.

"Working on it," Simon said shortly.

She couldn't resist a dig. "I'd imagine that even in a hospital like this, with its military affiliation, there are a lot of people—staff and patients—with agendas of their own. Secrets, or whatever. Not that I have any idea who the thieves were, but I don't think the investigation should just concentrate on people from the nearest Phoenix communities."

"You have reason to believe it was some kind of inside job?" Moe sounded incredulous. But why should he be surprised?

"I don't know, sir. But it never hurts to keep an open mind. As I said, secrets can exist anywhere." She aimed a look at Simon that bordered on accusation. "Now, if it's all right with you, I'd like to look at my new office, then start my rounds."

"What do you think, Parran?"

Simon dragged his gaze away from the retreating back of Grace Andreas and back to his boss.

"I think there's something she isn't telling us," Moe continued. "Do you agree?"

Simon agreed that Grace was hiding something in the obscurity of her comments. It was too much like the old days, when she had pushed to get him to blurt out things he didn't intend to say. She never succeeded.

She wouldn't succeed now, either. Even so, she had sounded somehow more sure of herself.

He needed to talk to her, see if his impression was right.

"I don't know," Simon told Moe. "I got the impression she was rattled by the theft, and the fact that she had come so close to catching the bad guys in the act. Maybe she's just scared." A good thing to tell Moe, he figured, but it wasn't the truth. Simon had detected irritation in Grace's attitude. Smugness and frustration, perhaps. But not fear.

"Maybe..." Moe sounded dubious.

"I've a case I'd like to consult with someone else on. I'll make it Dr. Andreas—and see if I can learn what she's really thinking."

"Go for it."

Simon actually did have a case he wanted another doctor's opinion about—especially Grace's.

The six-year-old son of an army private currently deployed overseas had been brought in with a nasty ear infection. Tests indicated it was strep, and the prescribed antibiotics, administered intravenously, seemed to be working well.

The kid, however, was not thriving in the hospital environment and was still too sick to go home. He turned away when nurses or physicians entered his room and refused to talk to anyone.

His mother visited but could not stay long. She was expecting another child, and hanging out in the Infectious Diseases Center was not a great idea. She'd told them that little Eddie was extremely shy. Patience was needed, and maybe some kind of diversion. She'd seen magicians and clowns on TV who sometimes visited kids in the hospital, and one of the other mothers had mentioned a dog who'd come in recently. Was something like that possible?

Simon had made no promises but said he'd see what he could do—a good reason to approach Grace.

He caught up with her in the hall, where her head was bent next to a nurse's over a chart. "May I speak with you, Dr. Andreas?"

"Sure. Hold on a moment, though."

While he waited, Simon inhaled her scent. It was softly floral and more, just as he'd remembered it from before and experienced it again since their reunion.

She finished her discussion with the nurse,

then looked at Simon. Did he detect a hint of trepidation?

"I'd like your help on a case," he said. "Room 2046." He explained the situation as he led her down the hall, passing nurses and visitors mostly going the other way. He stopped outside a nearby room. The odor from there suggested that the patient within had something dire going on. It wasn't his patient, though, but one being treated by another specialist. The smell wasn't heavy, perhaps not noticeable here without his enhanced senses.

Grace seemed to hesitate outside that door too. Interesting.

"Is it your patient in there?" he asked.

"I believe it's Dr. Scoles's. But—" She signaled to an approaching nurse. "I think I heard something in this room. Maybe one of the patients inside is vomiting. I'd suggest someone check."

Simon hadn't heard anything out of the ordinary, but at least the patient would get attention.

Why had Grace reacted that way? One more puzzle about her… Or was this just another way of goading—testing—him?

They soon reached the room that was their destination. "The patient's name is Eddie. He was too ill to put into the children's ward, although he's improving. But he needs some special cheering up, soon, if possible."

Grace peered inside. Simon saw that Eddie was asleep. "Let's not bother him now," Grace said. "But maybe we can work out some very special cheering up—like a doggy visit."

"Exactly what I was hoping you'd say." Simon grinned into those amazing sable eyes.

"Of course my dog and my friend Kristine's aren't the only canines around here." She was still looking into the room, past his shoulder. What was she talking about? Was it the same old teasing she'd done in the past?

Or was there something else on her mind?

He thought again about the canine presence he had sensed while he attempted to learn the fate of the shigellosis materials in a way no regular human could—with wolfen senses. He'd seen no further sign since then of the wolf he believed he had smelled and heard—unsurprising, of course, if it was wild.

Back in college, he hadn't pushed Grace as she had pushed him, even when she had hinted that she, too, was a shapeshifter. She had acted as if she was joking, and that was something he had learned to take very seriously after what had happened to his family.

But what if…? It would explain her reaction outside the room they had just passed.

Should he push the point now, or just pretend to play along with her?

Without really deciding, he heard himself ask, "How about joining me for dinner?"

"A date?" She sounded amused.

"A quick bite shared between colleagues to discuss a patient," he countered, figuring she was more likely to agree that way. "In the cafeteria."

"Sure," she said. "What time?"

Too easy, Grace thought. An opportunity to get Simon alone and talk to him?

Well, not exactly alone. They'd be surrounded by staff and visitors. She'd have to be careful what she said, not only to make sure she didn't annoy Simon too much to keep him from talking to her, but also to make sure no one eavesdropped on anything that shouldn't be overheard.

She arrived right on time. The cafeteria was large, with areas serving different kinds of foods as well as drinks. Since it was dinnertime, the place was crowded and noisy, but Grace's limited experience was that the staff was efficient and lines moved fast.

Simon was waiting near the entrance. "What are you in the mood for?" he asked. "Gourmet burgers, exotic salad?"

She laughed. "I'll have a mediocre deli sandwich. How about you?"

A short while later, they'd gotten their food and drinks, and sat at a table near a window.

"When can you visit Eddie with your dog?" Simon asked.

A neutral question, and she answered it neutrally, too. "Tomorrow or the next day. How long do you anticipate he'll be here?"

"At least another four or five days. With his mother expecting a little brother or sister, we want to make sure he's not contagious when he leaves."

"Right."

Grace watched Simon take a bite of his sandwich. How eating could look sexy, she didn't know. Or maybe his presence just kept reminding her of how he had looked naked…this time. His body was so much harder, more mature, than when they had been in college.

Involuntarily, her gaze traveled from his face down his chest, which was covered, unsurprisingly, by his buttoned white lab jacket.

She reminded herself of the circumstances that had led to her glimpsing the gorgeous body that lay beneath. She couldn't just let it go, even though she knew, from experience, what happened when she tried to get him to admit what he was.

And that was when she had only suspected the truth. Now, she *knew* it.

But how to get him to own up to it...?

The way she had gone about it when they were both in college hadn't worked then, and she doubted it would work now. Besides, back then she would have been able to admit the truth about herself if he had been honest with her. But now, she was an Alpha Force member, and nearly everything about the organization was highly classified—including the special abilities of its major operatives.

She decided to try sincerity, setting aside the pushiness generated by frustration that had governed her approach before. "It's really sweet of you to care about Eddie that way, Simon. I know how some patients can really get under our skin, make us care about them even more, somehow, than the other people we try to heal."

He nodded, his expression becoming grim. "I want to heal them all, damn it." He looked into her eyes as he shrugged his shoulders lightly. "I sound like some kind of save-the-world do-gooder, don't I, not just an ordinary physician who's dedicated but realistic."

One who just happens to be a shapeshifter—even when the moon wasn't full. That might be something else Simon dedicated himself to: figuring out some way of enhancing his abilities.

Had he also somehow enhanced the very human—sexy—abilities of his she had learned about in the old days? The idea sent a tickle of warmth through her insides that she ignored. That wasn't a distraction she needed.

"You seem both professional and caring to me—a good thing, Simon. You've impressed me so far." She took a sip of iced tea and let the cold, sweet liquid run down her throat while she thought of what to say next. When she glanced up, Simon was watching her, a hint of a smile curling his lips.

"Glad to hear it," he said. "I had the impression... Well, that our memories of the past were hanging over us, ready to interfere with our ability to work together now."

"I can deal with it," she said quickly. "How about you?"

"Definitely."

For a while, they discussed the Charles Carder facility in general, and how Simon had ended up here. "I did a lot of research, thought this place had a great reputation. I hadn't initially considered working in a military environment, but the fit made sense, so I applied and here I am."

Grace knew there had to be more to it than that. Had he chosen Arizona because wild wolves lived in the area so his being seen while shifted wouldn't draw undue attention? What else about this place had attracted him?

She could come right out and confront him. Tell him what she knew, what she had seen. Ask the underlying truths to all he said to her. But not here, even with the possibility being unlikely—in this large and noisy crowd—that anyone would be eavesdropping on them.

Besides, even if he admitted to being a shifter, that didn't preclude his having something to do with the theft of the biohazardous materials, as much as she hated to imagine the possibility. She had to do all she could to rule him out—or not—as part of her mission.

She pondered her next step. Why not be direct—about some questions, at least? "Do you have any ideas about who stole the biohazards?"

"No, but I wish I did. Infectious-disease specialists like us know too well what those kinds of materials could do in the wrong hands."

Grace nodded. "And since they were stolen, they're more likely to be in the possession of the worst kind of tangos—terrorists—than a little old lady who thought she was borrowing some kind of cleaning solution."

Simon's wry grin caused Grace to smile back as she watched him. They hadn't been talking suggestively. Their discussion had been on an especially serious topic. Even so, his expression grew hot as they looked at one another, and she knew hers did, as well.

He took a drink of his cola, his eyes not leaving hers. Waves of heat started pulsing inside her that had nothing to do with the Arizona temperatures outside. She tried to shake off her sense of wanting to touch him, and be touched.

Not an easy transition while looking at the man who had driven her so crazy with lust all those years ago. But maybe she could use their attraction to take a look around his quarters, see if she could find any answers there.

Then leave, fast, before she did something she would regret. Not that she had ever regretted making love with Simon before—only its aftermath.

"I've had enough to eat," she said. "I wouldn't mind a glass of wine somewhere quiet, though. Do you happen to have any at your place?"

"Sure do." The huskiness in his voice was also tinged with surprise.

"Do you live in one of those really nice, upscale residential buildings at the other side of campus? I've heard that most of the nonmilitary doctors have apartments there, even if they've got another home somewhere. It helps having a place to catch some sleep after busy days and nights on duty. I've been hoping to see what the apartments look like."

"Yes, I've got a place," Simon told her, "and I'd be happy to give you a tour."

Chapter 6

Was he nuts?

Getting involved again with Grace was way off his agenda. Simon knew that as well as he knew his own name.

Although in her presence, after that suggestive look they'd shared that had gotten the attention of some of his most critical body parts, he might have stumbled over his name if asked to identify himself.

The walk from the hospital, where the cafeteria was located, to one of the farthest reaches of the property comprising the Charles Carder facility should have cooled him off, but it didn't.

He tried to blame it on the desert heat, even now, after sundown, yet he knew better.

They walked along the wide path lined by drought-tolerant plants that dotted the sand. They didn't touch at all, which was a good thing. If Simon had felt even the warmth from Grace's body from her shoulder brushing his arm, he'd have to fight the urge to grab her, kiss her—hell, do even more here, in the open, with the few other pedestrians on the pathway observing them.

When they reached his building, he grabbed his security key, but Grace had stopped on the pathway and was staring at the structure. "Nice place. A lot better outside, at least, than the boxy quarters on the air-force base."

"Supposedly, the original Charles Carder, a doctor who retired from the military and started this place, paid to have an architect design all the structures here."

"I do see some similarities to the hospital's style. Which wing do you live in?"

He pointed off to their right. "Sixth floor."

She glanced at him. "If you were out on your balcony last night, you might have seen some of what went on around the storage and incineration building." Her expression was keen yet mocking. Why? She couldn't know where he had really been during most of that night—but it was definitely far from his balcony and the rest of the building.

"Unfortunately, I wasn't watching." Not from here, at least.

She waited a second before turning her head and striding up to the front door. He obliged by opening it, then took her elbow to lead her through the large entryway with its conversation pit where light brown upholstered chairs formed a semicircle, past a few potted plants, and to the elevator bank. He pushed the up button—and removed his hand from her arm. The current that had leaped through him at the contact seemed more than electric.

At least there hadn't been anyone else downstairs or in the elevator. People here tended to be friendly, and Simon wasn't in the mood for long introductions and idle chatter.

When they arrived on the sixth floor, he gestured toward the open elevator door. "This is it."

Grace preceded him out and waited for him to lead her. "This way." He pointed to the right, trying to stay casual even as he wanted to pick her up and carry her fast down the wide, lighted hallway.

When they were inside his apartment, he shut the door, then turned toward her. Oh, yes. He wanted her. Bad. Yet he wasn't about to rush her. Assuming she even wanted what he did. But why else would she be here?

As she had downstairs, she looked around. "I like it." He tried to see the place through her eyes. The entry opened into a recessed living room, and the hallway to the two bedrooms was off to the left. The walls were bland and white, but he'd hung photos he had taken of local desert scenes. His furniture was sparse but comfortable. The kitchen door was off the side of the living room.

"Tour first, or wine?" he asked.

"Tour. Is that the balcony?" She pointed to a sliding glass door in the living room.

"Right."

She headed there, and he accompanied her, opening the door. The Charles Carder campus was well lighted even though it was dark outside, and he could see part of the building where the hazardous materials were to be stored and destroyed, just beyond a parking lot behind the looming hospital structure.

"Yes, too bad you weren't up here looking out," she said again, then stared up at him in the artificial light he had turned on. She seemed to study his face. No sign of sexual interest in her expression now.

It was as though she was searching him,

trying to find out just by watching what his subliminal thoughts were.

That was easy. He wanted her.

"Yeah, too bad," he agreed. He stepped toward her and took her into his arms. She didn't back off, but neither did she react as he'd hoped—like grabbing him and starting to tear his clothes off.

Instead, she continued to look at him. "Do you ever see any wildlife from here? We're far enough from Phoenix that I bet there are some interesting populations."

Was this her way of leading back into the discussions that had driven them apart before?

"Do you want to know how many owls and roadrunners I've glimpsed around here?" He didn't try to hide his irritation. "Coyotes, maybe? Or wolves? I thought I saw a couple of them in the distance, too. Why? Do you think there are shapeshifters?" He inserted scorn into his voice. If they were going to dredge up old differences, they might as well get it out now. Although he'd really been looking forward to sex with Grace—again.

"Maybe I do," she said softly. "Maybe I saw one." But before he could respond she reached up and drew his face down closer to hers.

And then her lips were playing hot, seeking

games with his, and any sarcastic—or defensive—response he might dream up was suddenly toast.

This wasn't what she had planned. Grace was not an impulsive person. She had anticipated that Simon might touch her. Hold her. Even kiss her. She had intended to respond cordially, showing some interest but not leaping into bed with him.

She had barely started the recon she had intended to do here, looking for clues about who Simon really was, whether he could have stolen the biohazards, how he had shifted outside of a full moon without being part of Alpha Force.

But though all that flashed through her mind now, it disappeared in a storm of sexual lightning as hot as the real thing. Her body had reacted to his touch, no matter what her mind had intended. And now she was definitely engaged in his torrid embrace.

Simon's mouth seared hers, even as his tongue teased in small thrusts that suggested what the stiff erection she could feel against her would do once they were off the balcony, in his place, out of their impeding clothes.

She wanted that to happen. Longed for it, even edged her body back toward the door that would take them inside.

Simon needed no further prompting. In moments, they were in his living room, the patio door closed, the slatted shades drawn, and she was pulling at the buttons of his shirt.

Her T-shirt was suddenly gone, as quickly as if it had evaporated in the heat outside. Her bra, too, and she gasped as the palm of one of Simon's hands rubbed gently but firmly against one nipple, then the other, springing them to full attention.

His shirt was off now, and Grace managed to pull away long enough to glimpse again his hard, muscular chest. She used the opportunity to reach down to his zipper—but that was unnecessary since Simon suddenly stepped out of his pants. His boxers, too. His nudity was familiar, but now that he was so close it was like experiencing the view of him for the first time in years, and Grace nearly cried out in her need.

He had gotten the rest of her clothes off, too. "Show me your bedroom," she managed to gasp.

"Too far." He responded by moving her sideways as he remained against her, toward the nearby sofa.

He laid her down upon it first, and she pulled him with her, managing to maneuver her hand between them so she could touch, then stroke, his large, hard erection.

He groaned, even as he touched her between her legs, causing her to gasp once more.

She heard the crackling of a plastic wrapper.

Where had he found a condom? But she felt an instant of relief and pride in him. He'd already indicated that he was a responsible doctor. Clearly it was true…and the protection could prevent a lot of unwanted complications.

And then he was inside her, hot and moving and driving her to the pinnacle of arousal that she remembered from so long ago.

"Simon," she cried, even as she reached her climax and heard him call her name, too, as he soared into his own release.

"Déjà vu," Grace said into Simon's shoulder as she finally caught her breath. "Or something like that. Wow."

"'Wow' is a good description." His voice was raspy, and his breath lifted her hair as he spoke.

"I guess some things don't change. Although—"

"Although this time, let's do it in a more comfortable place. Care to see my bedroom?"

She absolutely did. And, yes, some things didn't change. Way back when, Simon's stamina and abilities for multiple sex acts had amazed her.

She suspected he was about to amaze her, again.

He did.

A while later, Grace lay beside Simon in his

king-size bed, the blue, silky sheets and patterned coverlet strewn around them. Her back was to him, and she lay against him as one of his arms held her close.

She felt thoroughly sated. Happy. Exhausted.

Yet frustrated, too. Not sexually. Definitely not sexually. But she hadn't come up with a casual, nonconfrontational way to tell Simon what she knew about him.

Making love with a shifter was no different, while they were in human form, from having sex with a regular person without those abilities. She knew. She'd had a few short relationships after Simon, but none had amounted to anything.

Only—well, that was true as to the mechanics, but not otherwise. Not with Simon. His lovemaking had always been extraordinary. It still was.

But it didn't reveal his shapeshifting side.

Plus, although she wanted to clear Simon completely from any suspicion in the theft of the biohazards, she couldn't, yet. Yes, it was unlikely that he could have gassed the guards and taken anything while in wolf form, but she had no idea when, and how, he had changed. Maybe he'd decided to shift to observe the area from which he had stolen the hazardous materials. He obviously had a way of changing outside the full moon, and she had no idea of the parameters of his method.

But if he had stolen them, why would he have done it? He had shown his compassionate side over and over. It would be more in character for him to leave the materials there, to be incinerated the next morning.

Or was that the character she ascribed to him because she wanted to?

Simon's breathing had deepened beside her. He was asleep.

Maybe now was a good time for her to do her recon, see if there was anything to be seen— good or bad—in Simon's apartment.

Slowly, she untangled herself from him and from the bedclothes. If he awoke and asked what she was doing, she would just say she needed a trip to the bathroom. She'd noticed one across the hall from this bedroom.

Instead, she edged her way into the living room, listening for any indication that Simon was stirring. She found her purse and sent a quick text message to Kristine, letting her aide know she was working and wouldn't be home until very late that night, if at all. She could explain—some of it—later.

Next, she took a brief look around the living room and kitchen areas, not expecting to find anything useful. She slipped on her underwear, which remained in a heap with the rest of her clothes on the floor, uncomfortable about sneaking around the place nude.

She had noticed a door to what appeared to be another bedroom near the room where Simon was, and that was where she went next. If he had a home office, that was likely to be it—which it was.

She wished she had a flashlight, but instead there was a lamp on the desk that she turned on after closing the door behind her.

She wasn't sure what she was looking for. If she was certain he'd stay asleep, she would boot up Simon's desktop computer and see what files were there. Maybe check out his e-mail if he hadn't logged off. But if he woke and came in here, it would be obvious that she had violated his privacy.

Instead, she slowly opened the drawers in his desk and glanced inside. It wasn't likely he'd have hard copies of any correspondence that described his intent to steal biohazard samples, but maybe there'd be something from his family that hinted at his shifter background.

The better thing to do might be to "borrow" Simon's apartment key and send Kristine here sometime to hack into the computer. She'd be good at something like that. For now, snooping into the drawers had yielded Grace nothing useful. All she'd seen so far was personal bookkeeping materials, some medical journals, and—

"Hey. What are you doing, Grace?" The door had opened, and the overhead office light flicked on.

She jumped, startled, and closed the drawer she'd been surveying on her hand—not hard, fortunately. She pulled it free quickly and lifted her bruised fingers to her mouth. "Oh. I didn't want to wake you, but I was looking for…a pen and paper. I wanted to start a to-do list, with bringing Tilly to meet that boy Eddie at the top." Lame, but it was the best she could think of that fast. "I'd gotten up for a bathroom break, and—"

"What the hell is this, Grace? I want to know the truth. Come with me."

He had pulled on his boxers, limiting her view, but the parts of his otherwise unclothed body that were visible still made her remember—and react. As they got into the hall, her gaze slid toward the door to his bedroom. But he was leading her the other way.

"We never did get any wine," he said, striding away from her. "Now's as good a time as any."

Wine? In the middle of the night? She didn't want her mind any muzzier than it was.

But going along with him—as much as possible—might help to take the sting out of the inevitable confrontation between them. She grabbed the rest of her clothes and got dressed, then followed him into the kitchen.

There, he opened a bottle of merlot that he pulled from a wine rack beside the refrigerator and poured some into long-stemmed glasses. The action seemed out of sync with reality, an attempt at being courteous while all etiquette had been discarded. Even so, Grace accepted the glass and took a sip.

"Sit down," Simon ordered, pointing toward the small oval table in the middle of the room. Chairs on wheels had been pushed under it, and he pulled one out for her.

She didn't obey. Standing, preparing to flee, felt more appropriate.

"This wine is good," she said. "It has a slightly nutty essence, and—"

"What is really going on, Grace? What were you looking for?"

The fury on the gorgeous male face that had so recently looked at her with lust-provoking heat made tears rush to her eyes. She blinked them back, modifying her own purposely bland expression into one of chilly observation. "All right." She finally took the seat that he had offered to her. "I'll tell you the little that

I can. I am a medical doctor, as you know—an infectious-disease specialist, and I'm also in the military. What you don't know is that I am in a special ops unit that has been designated to look into the thefts of biohazards here at Charles Carder." That was as much as Colonel Otis had been told, somewhat classified but not at all as secret as the true nature of Alpha Force.

"I get it." Simon took a large swig of his wine, then returned to glaring at her. "And you somehow think that I'm involved?"

"I don't want to think so, but I'm not sure," she said honestly. "Simon, I saw you the other night, after the theft—walking by the parking lot near the storage and incineration building." She couldn't bring herself to confront him now about his shapeshifting just before the time she mentioned. That might follow, but she so much wanted him to admit it to her first. "I have to include you in my investigation. Please, give me any evidence, any proof you have, about what you were doing before that, and why you couldn't be the thief."

Chapter 7

Simon had no proof. He resented that Grace even asked for it. At least she had apparently seen him late enough that he had already shifted back to human form. Otherwise, she would have said something about seeing a wolf—or seeing him change.

He got up for the bottle of wine, needing more—especially with that image in his mind: Grace, seeing him shifting. As he sat again, he studied her face. Beautiful, but unreadable.

What was she thinking?

Whatever it was, he needed to respond to her. "I shouldn't have to defend myself to you," he asserted. "I didn't steal those damned bio-hazards. Why would I?"

"I don't know," she said softly. "Just tell me why you were in that area then. What you were doing. Please, Simon."

Her expression turned imploring. But he wasn't about to tell her what she asked—at least not all of it.

She wasn't pushing, goading him to admit he was a shapeshifter, as she did in the old days. Wouldn't she be doing that if she knew the truth? Or did she have a different agenda now?

Back then, the pain his family had suffered was too raw for him to admit to anyone what he was, even someone he had cared about as he'd done with Grace.

She had hinted then that she, too, was a shapeshifter, a werewolf, daring him to admit that he also could morph that way. But he had trusted no one, not even the woman he had formed a relationship with. Just as well, since the relationship had proven to be tenuous.

She hadn't insinuated that she could be a shifter now, though. Whatever her reasons back then, her hints could not have been true. She was in the military, some special investigatory troop, so she couldn't possibly be anything but a regular person. Otherwise, someone would have found out—during training, on missions, whatever—especially since, as far as he had determined after long efforts at research, no other shifter besides him, and the few family members he had occasionally allowed to test his formulations, could avoid changing, even for a while, under a full moon.

Now she might not be eager to tease him about what she'd probably been kidding about back then, irrational woo-woo stuff, at least to her.

What she hinted at could be even more serious.

And, damn it all, her suspicions hurt. Especially after they had made love so enthusiastically.

A thought penetrated his skull, generating so much pain that he stood, draining his wine glass. "Did you come here with me last night just so you could snoop around, look for evidence that I'm some kind of terrorist, Grace? One who would resort to stealing biohazards that might be used to kill people, rather than cure them? Did you use sex as your ticket to get in here?"

She stood, too, so fast that her chair rocketed out behind her on its wheels. "How can you ask something like that? I came here because…because I'm still too damned attracted to you. I don't want to believe the worst about you. I need some answers, yes, but I came here because I wanted to make love with you. And because I was hoping—still hope—that you'll stop keeping secrets from me. Tell me the truth."

"Which you think is that I'm a thief or worse?"

"No, damn it. I want you to tell me—"

"What I'll tell you is that it's time for you to leave, Grace. It's been fun. You're still one hot lady. But like before, as soon as we start talking instead of having sex, things go to hell. I'll walk you back to your place."

"Don't bother. I'm a lot better prepared to take care of myself than you are. I'm a highly trained military operative. You're only a man with one huge…ego." She slammed her wine glass back onto the table so hard that he thought she'd broken the stem, although it still looked intact.

Then she stormed out of his apartment.

Damn the arrogant, secretive, lying SOB!

In her mind, Grace dared anyone to approach her as she walked along the lighted paths across the Charles Carder campus and back toward her quarters on the air-force base. She was ready to kick some serious butt. Strangle someone.

Most of all, she wanted to throttle Simon.

She had made it so easy for him to disclose what he was. She shouldn't have to reveal that she knew the truth about him. He should just tell her. They'd had sex again, hadn't they? Gotten close once more. And now he was just acting defensive.

Well, she had all but called him a thief, and of something that could label him a terrorist if her allegation was true.

Grace started to calm down as she approached the gate between the two facilities. She could understand his fury about that—if it wasn't just an act.

What would she do if—when—Simon finally told her what he was? Throw herself back into his arms and say she had always wanted to find a werewolf to care for? Make love with?

If he asked why, she would have to lie to him—as he was lying to her. Or at least misdirecting her, hiding the truth. She might have a reason that was in the interest of national security, but it would be a lie nonetheless.

She sighed as she walked up to the boxy building that housed her apartment. Things could never be open and aboveboard between Simon and her. Hoping for his confession was a major reason why she had gone with him to his place that night—his confession to being a werewolf, like her.

Not his confession to having anything to do with the biohazards thefts.

Despite his having been in the area at the right time, she didn't actually believe he could be guilty of that—even if he hadn't yet shifted. She would most likely defend him if anyone accused him—unless, of course, they had irrefutable evidence otherwise.

She entered the building and walked up the steps to her unit, needing the exercise to blow off the excess energy from her now-dissipating anger.

Despite how late it was, Grace sat in her small living room half an hour later with the rest of her Alpha Force team, along with Tilly and Bailey. Autumn Kater's cover animal, the red-tailed hawk Venus, was present, too, in a small cage designed for portability. She had a much larger one in Autumn's quarters, but was most often left free inside that space. She was well trained, and remained as unfettered as possible.

No wine was present, and the wee hours of the morning were not a good time for coffee, in case anyone harbored any hope of catching another hour or two of sleep. Grace had put out glasses of ice water for the humans, plus a bowl for the dogs to share. Autumn would need to provide Venus with anything she needed.

"Any more information on the driver of that delivery car?" Grace asked.

Grace knew Autumn. Trusted her integrity and intelligence. If the guy's leaving with something other than what he went in with made Autumn suspicious, then it had been a suspicious act.

"Not enough, damn it." Autumn stood from the stiff-backed chair she had chosen and began to pace the small room. She was slender and not very tall, and with long arms that Grace could visualize morphing into wings. Her hair was brown with red highlights, and the length of her nose vaguely suggested a beak. But it was her dark, penetrating eyes that looked most hawk-like, appearing to see everything. "I've been looking into it more, but they've been cagey with their responses. They've not disclosed a good reason for the guy to have taken beer away from the site."

"My bet is that it was a different brand than the pizza place usually sold and the guy was having a party," Ruby said. "The guards probably knew the delivery guy. Got invited to his party as long as they supplied some beer."

"Maybe," Grace said. "But it could have

been a planned diversion. And next time, assuming there is a next time—"

"I'll just be a good little raptor," Autumn affirmed, "and watch what's going on below me. Let someone else follow anyone suspicious."

"Like maybe a wolf," Grace said, smiling. "Especially if the real security guys don't do what they're supposed to."

"Kristine said that you shifted, too, after the theft," Autumn said. "Did you see anything interesting?"

Grace wished that her fellow Alpha Force members would stop asking her that, no matter how appropriate it was. "Nothing that would help identify the thief," she answered.

"And tonight," Ruby said. "You were with that other infectious-diseases specialist, right? Kristine said you might have seen him wandering around after the theft occurred. Do you think he was involved?"

Grace hadn't given Kristine any details— especially not the most important one. But her aide knew that, whatever she had been doing this night, it had to involve the matter they were investigating, at least peripherally. Grace had decided not to try to sneak Kristine into Simon's apartment to try to hack his computer. Too many further complications if she was caught.

Or if she did find proof of what Simon was. No, Grace wanted to be the only one to uncover that.

"My current belief is that he might have been conducting his own investigation," Grace said. He hadn't said so, but that would explain why he happened to have shifted that night—assuming he had control over it without a full moon. Maybe she could get him to confirm he was looking into the thefts, at least.

"So he's not a person of interest?" Kristine asked.

I wouldn't say that, Grace thought. But to her Alpha Force comrades she said, "To my knowledge, he wasn't the thief, just a doctor concerned about the biohazard samples after the prior thefts."

"With good reason," Kristine said.

"True," Grace responded, then moved their conversation—but not her thoughts—away from Simon.

At 1300 hours, Grace walked down a hall toward the office of Major Louis Dryson. He was the commanding officer of the Air Force Security Forces stationed at the Zimmer Air Force Base, now assigned also to handle security at Charles Carder—the person she had mentioned to Drew Connell as someone she wanted to speak with.

She'd set her alarm to awaken her at 0800 so she could call early and set up this appointment, and had stayed up long enough to take Tilly for a short walk. Then she went back to bed.

Not that she had slept much. She kept rehashing her time with Simon last night—both the extraordinarily good and the ill-tempered bad. Despite anticipating a somewhat unpleasant face-off with Major Dryson, she looked forward even less to the next time she saw Simon. There was bound to be a further confrontation.

Which would hurt all the more now that they'd shared such a wonderful time in bed—before all hell had broken loose between them. Again.

She reached the major's office. A woman with the insignia of a master sergeant on her camo uniform sat behind the desk in the outer office. She looked up as Grace entered. "Lt. Andreas?" she asked.

"That's right."

"Major Dryson is expecting you." She stood, opened the door behind her and announced Grace's presence.

The man in a similar uniform who stood behind a much larger desk was broad and barrel-chested. He gestured impatiently for Grace to enter, as if he had ordered her appearance and she was late. "Have a seat, lieutenant." As Grace complied, he continued, "Colonel Otis at the hospital asked that I cooperate with you, so tell me what you need from me." His tone suggested that the last thing he wanted was to do anything for her, but he watched her expectantly, hazel eyes frowning beneath thick glasses.

Grace wasn't about to play his game. She took a moment to look around his small, neat office, her gaze lighting on his desktop computer and files stacked nearby. There was nothing unusual or especially enlightening about the room or its contents, but she took her time before returning her gaze to Dryson's.

"As the colonel may have told you, I'm here on a special assignment to find out who is stealing biohazard specimens at Charles Carder and help to apprehend them. I assume that's your intention, too, so I believe it's in our best interests to pool any information we have."

"Then do you have any information to share with me, lieutenant?"

"Probably nothing you don't already know, since your unit is conducting the official investigation into the incident that occurred the other night. You've probably investigated some of the earlier thefts as well."

"I assume you thought you could just buzz in here," he said scornfully, "figure out what was going on and take credit for capturing our thieves. Was that why you hadn't come to talk to me before this?"

In a way, that was true. Whatever their mission, the local security forces had been ineffective in stopping the thefts and arresting the perpetrators, so their value was already suspect.

Even more, keeping Alpha Force and its presence here low-key was paramount to its effectiveness—and to ensuring that its covert nature remained secret.

"Sorry, sir, but I only arrived a few days ago, and I needed to establish my cover at the hospital facility. I actually am a medical doctor, specializing in infectious diseases. That was one reason why I was chosen for this particular assignment."

"And your unit—Alpha Force, isn't it? That's what the colonel said." The colonel should have been more discreet, not even giving out the name of her unit. "It has some better plan for catching our tangos?"

"Although it's a good possibility, we're not sure our targets are terrorists, sir. In any event, we knew this assignment wasn't going to be a slam-dunk, but our team members work separately from other units with the same goal as we have."

"Why is that?" He had stood, and his expression was even more belligerent, as if he intended to attack Grace for not buckling under his command.

"As Colonel Otis may have told you, sir, our unit is covert, and so is how we conduct our operations. As much as we want to achieve the objective of fixing this potentially critical situation, we have to handle it our way, just as you have to handle it your way. We don't currently have any genuine suspects, but if that changes we'll let you know. How about you? Are there any suspects currently on your radar that we should know about?"

His sudden grin was as disconcerting as his scowl had been. "We're checking into the viability of several people seen near the storage building that night as suspects. You're one of them, lieutenant. So is Sgt. Norwood, and I understand she's part of your team. A couple of others, too—a few doctors, some hospital visitors, a delivery guy…but so far no one sticks out as being more than just a person of interest."

A few doctors. Did that include Simon? Had

anyone else seen him in wolf form—or changing? Unlikely. Grace hadn't seen or otherwise sensed anyone else nearby then. But he could have been seen before or afterward in human form.

Maybe she should warn him. That might only cause another argument between them—if she told him she wasn't the only one who needed to clear him. But candor in this, at least, was possible and could help him. This major might not only glom on to Simon as his main suspect, but might also ignore better ones if he could more easily pin the theft on Simon.

She had intended to talk to Simon later anyway. Set up a time to bring Tilly back to the hospital to visit with his young patient as well as act as a diversion for more kids, seniors and psychiatric patients again…as her ongoing excuse to visit other areas of the hospital where infectious-disease specialists might not otherwise go.

She'd be cautious about how to let Simon know of this additional suspicion against him. But it was important—especially because he was a shifter. If anyone besides her found out, the repercussions could be horrific.

"Here's my card with my cell phone number, major," Grace said, taking it from her pocket. "I'll stay in touch with you, but if you find yourself focusing on any particular suspects, I'd appreciate your letting me know. Our respective superior officers will, too." She threw that in to make sure this difficult man remembered that they both held positions in the military and were under orders to figure this out.

But he could never know what her specific orders, and abilities, happened to be.

Chapter 8

Grace watched for Simon for the rest of the day, but only saw him at a distance, or in a patient's room. He seemed to be avoiding her.

She wished that didn't hurt so much.

But pain or not, she had to talk to him. To warn him. He might not be high on her suspect list, but he could be on Dryson's—and if Simon was under surveillance, he might get caught by someone in authority, and even on camera, doing something he clearly wanted no one to know about.

How different today was from yesterday, when Grace was full of anticipation about meeting Simon for dinner—and hoping to get him alone to sound him out about the night of the thefts. And, okay, she admitted to herself that she had also wanted to get him alone for other reasons.

Reasons that had gone way beyond her expectations. Making love with Simon once more had been an experience she would relive over and over in her mind—and her sated body— even if it never happened again.

That was part of her pain, even though—or maybe because—she knew it was reality.

But even so, she cared enough to pass along her warning, then leave him alone, the way he clearly wanted. She allowed her most canine senses leeway to find him that day—the distant sound of his voice, his masculine scent wafting among all the usual hospital aromas. She finally got to the point that she delayed seeing a patient of her own to wait for Simon in the hallway, after seeing him enter a room to check on one of his patients—that boy, Eddie.

Was she stalking Simon? In a way. He shot a glare at her as he came out, talking to a nurse.

"May I speak with you, Dr. Parran?" she called.

"Sorry," he muttered, sounding not at all sorry. "I have to follow up on this now, Dr. Andreas. I'll talk to you later."

But Grace knew he intended that to be a lie. Shades of their college days all over again.

For now, she gave up. One way or another, she would catch up with Simon before this day ended and pass along the warning. For his sake.

And then?

Then, she would back off the way she never had in the old days—until they had given up on each other. Despite the wonders they had shared the night before, she was older now, and wiser.

Simon Parran and she would never have a relationship of any kind besides a professional one.

She would live with that. The pain she felt now was acute, but it would soften with time, as it had before. Eventually.

But if there was any way of learning how Simon had shifted outside the full moon, she owed it to Alpha Force to do so.

His duties at the hospital had ended for the day, and Simon looked around before heading along the now-quiet hall on the hospital's first floor, toward the stairway to the downstairs lab area. It was time now for him to get back to his extracurricular activities.

He wished he could return to them with the same enthusiasm he'd had previously. But too many things had happened to interfere with all he had intended to achieve here at Charles Carder.

The biohazards thefts, for one thing. He'd known of the prior ones, but they had been surpassed by the latest event. Having this severe strain of shigella bacteria in the wrong hands was a potential disaster. And so far, he had been unable to do anything about it.

Then there was Grace. He'd had a hell of a time concentrating on being a doctor that day instead of a man ruled by his private parts.

He had seen her around even before she had waited to talk to him outside Eddie's room. Smelled her light floral aroma at a distance, too. It mesmerized him, engulfed his senses, sparked recollections of the greatest aspects of the night before.

That aroma seemed to follow him everywhere. He passed a few visitors, an orderly, some maintenance workers as he walked along, yet he scented Grace—or imagined he did. He reached the door to the stairs and took the knob in his hand…and then realized it wasn't his imagination after all. Grace was hurrying along the hall toward him, the muted sound of the treads of her soft-soled shoes squishing along the linoleum.

No good way to avoid her now. He wasn't

about to hurry down the stairway—especially since she was likely to follow. "Hi, Grace," he said as she caught up with him. He purposely made his tone stiff, unwelcoming.

She obviously recognized that, since a brief cloud of emotion—pain?—washed over her face before she regained a neutral expression. "Hello, Simon. I know you're not interested in talking to me, but I did want to touch base with you about bringing Tilly for a session with your young patient." She leaned toward him, and her scent wafted over him like a soft, caressing shower. "There's something else you need to know, too." A couple of hospital visitors passed by, talking quietly and not looking at them, but Grace glanced in their direction. "Can we go someplace more private to talk?" she asked softly.

She glanced toward the door where he had stopped. He wasn't about to suggest that she accompany him down to the lab area. She might expect an invitation into the room where he worked. "How about my office upstairs?"

His office was near Grace's—an equally small one with a computer for checking patient records and communicating with other physicians by e-mail and phone. He could talk to Grace there behind closed doors—although he doubted that was a good idea. Maybe he could use the department lounge instead. Moe Scoles and his assistant would probably be gone for the day, and not many other doctors or staff were likely to be present either.

They took the stairs at the end of the hall up to the second floor and walked nearly silently toward the infectious-diseases wing. Simon peered into the department lounge before gesturing for Grace to precede him in there. "I'd like a cola," he said, heading for the soft-drink machine in the corner of the small room furnished with a few aging chairs of mismatched green-and-yellow slipcovers. "Want anything?" He wasn't really thirsty, but that gave him a reason to enter the lounge without explaining to Grace that he wanted to be somewhere from which he could leave more easily than his office if their conversation was as difficult as he anticipated.

"No, thanks."

He slipped some coins in and heard the resulting thunk of the can he had chosen rolling out of its chute. Grace had taken a seat on a chair with another close by, perpendicular to it. She motioned for him to sit there.

"Look, Grace," he said as he sat. "I really regret that we had such a nasty end to a...well, remarkable night. Being with you was—"

"No need to try to smooth things over,

Simon. I didn't want to speak with you to rehash it. The sex was great, our argument sucked, and that's that."

Her lovely face had taken on a hard expression. That should have made him feel relieved that they were simply moving on, but instead he had to quash an unanticipated ache inside.

"There are two things we need to discuss," she continued. "First, unless you have any objections, I'll bring Tilly in tomorrow afternoon to do another therapy-dog exercise. We'll be sure to visit your patient Eddie, see if his shyness is eased a little if a very smart dog gives him attention, okay?"

"Fine. Are you on duty at all tomorrow?"

"In the morning for a few hours, then I'm officially off for the day. This should work out fine."

"Good."

The remote look on her face grew suddenly uncertain. "There's something else you should know."

He had the impression he wasn't going to like it, whatever it was.

She hesitated, looking around the room, including toward the ceiling, as if checking for security cameras. "I need to go to my office," she said. "Please walk with me."

Whatever was on her mind, she obviously

didn't want anyone else to hear. Were there cameras recording what went on in the doctors' lounge? He doubted it, but rose and followed her.

She stopped in the hall, putting her hand partly over her mouth, as if to hide it from any prying camera lens. "I'm going to speak quietly." Her voice was barely above a whisper. He wondered if he would be able to hear it if he had strictly human hearing and leaned down as if needing the additional closeness to make out what she said. "Simon, I'm not the only one considering you a suspect in the biohazards theft. I'm convinced you're innocent, but Major Dryson of the Air Force Security Forces has you on his radar. You may be under close scrutiny. Very close scrutiny. And we both know what a bad thing that could be for you. Be really careful, Simon, about what you do and where you do it."

Shocked, he backed up. Was she telling him that she now really knew he was a shifter—and that the surveillance being conducted by the security group could reveal that about him if he didn't take precautions?

"Grace, I'd like to talk to you more about this. Somewhere else, if possible."

"Like your apartment, or mine, one of these

nights? I don't think so, Simon. Just be careful."
She turned and walked toward the stairway.

As he sat in the busy hospital cafeteria that
evening, nibbling on a sandwich and watching
the other diners—Grace not among them—Simon's frustration was palpable.

Not just his sexual frustration, although he
did regret not anticipating an encore session
with Grace. Yes, he'd been peeved with her
and her suspiciousness. But he could live with
that, especially since it sounded as if she was
now convinced of his innocence.

Was she also convinced he was a shapeshifter? Was that the hidden meaning behind
her warning? She was no longer pushing him
to admit it as she had when they were college
kids—yet he wasn't sure that she no longer suspected him of it.

The way she cautioned him seemed suspicious in itself.

Although she had hinted back then that she,
too, was a shifter, she wasn't doing so now. Was
that because she was a regular human, or because she didn't want him to know the truth?

Could she have been the canine presence he
had noticed while he, too, was shifted?

If he came right out and asked her, he would
have to admit what he was, too—and he still

wasn't ready to do that. Plus, he sensed she'd be the one to get defensive now, and deny it, whether or not it was true.

Yeah, he was frustrated. And those weren't the only reasons.

He'd also had to limit his activities on the lab floor. Working on his homeopathic and herbal remedies was no problem. But if what Grace said was true, he was under closer scrutiny now. Working on the formulations he really wanted to, experimenting and blending for his own tests— that might not be reasonable at the moment.

"Hello, Simon. Would you mind some company?" It was Grace.

She held a cup of coffee. He hadn't seen her because his back was toward the large coffee urns.

"Please, join me." He pointed across the table.

"Thanks." She sat and regarded him with an expression so sad that he fought an urge to stand and take her into his arms. "I didn't mean to alarm you before. Or to make old wounds between us start festering by pushing you last night. I…well, I enjoyed what we started between us again. I'm sorry it can't continue."

"It could," he suggested, keeping his face somber instead of letting it light up into a hopeful smile.

"There's too much baggage between us, Simon. The old attraction is still there, and maybe even more now. But…well, when I saw you here alone I couldn't resist coming over to talk to you. As impossible as it may seem, I'd like for us to be friends, as well as colleagues. Can we try that for now?"

"Maybe, but—" He couldn't resist. He leaned toward her over the table, making sure first that no one was near enough to hear over the crowd's roar what he was about to say. "My turn to ask you," he said softly. "Grace, are you a shapeshifter?"

Her lovely brown eyes widened, as if in shock. And then she burst out laughing. "After all that I put you through in the old days, Simon, and after expressing my suspicions against you today, I shouldn't be surprised that you'd try to get back at me now. See you tomorrow." She grabbed her coffee cup, stood and hurried away through the crowd.

Leaving Simon realizing that she hadn't answered his question any more than he'd answered hers back in the day.

Grace should be laughing for real over this irony—not the feigned laugh she had shot at Simon.

Oh, how the tables had turned, she thought

as she hurried across the hospital parking lot toward the air-force base's gate. Now she should simply avoid Simon and fulfill her mission as quickly as she could. She had already come up with some ideas to run by her fellow Alpha Force members here before trying them on Major Drew Connell. Ideas that might bring the thieves into the open so she could catch them in the act.

But despite herself, she was worried about Simon, and whether he could keep his true nature secret while the investigation into the biohazards thefts continued. She had the resources of Alpha Force to help protect her and the other side of her nature. As far as she knew, Simon was on his own.

The night air was stifling as usual. Even so, Grace especially looked forward to being with Tilly that night. She had a lot to think about, and the calming presence of her dog, as well as the brisk exercise of a long walk around the base even under bright artificial lights, might help her figure out her next moves.

Which, regretfully, wouldn't include another passionate night with Simon Parran.

Chapter 9

"So what's your great idea?" Autumn Katers asked Grace. The four Alpha Force members were back in Grace's quarters that night. She had contacted the others after her walk with Tilly and said she needed their opinion about something important.

Now they all sipped lemonade that Grace had asked Kristine to bring in for them. The two dogs sat on the floor at their feet, and Autumn's alter-ego hawk Venus was present in her cage again, too. It rested on the clunky coffee table they had gathered around.

"I'm eager for things to move faster," Grace said, without any intention of explaining why she wanted to fulfill her mission and move on as quickly as possible. It was becoming much too hurtful to stay around Simon.

Although if they all bought into her idea and it worked, that still wouldn't resolve her other dilemma of finding the key to Simon's shifting abilities. She had done some subtle checking, and neither he nor anyone related to him had apparently ever been associated with Alpha Force. Maybe he was friends with a member of the team, but that hadn't shown up either. So far, Grace had found no indication that anyone had handed Simon a sample of the Alpha Force shifting elixir. Nor did he seem to have any knowledge of what Alpha Force was about.

No, whatever he was doing to control his shifts, it had to be devised by him. Or at least not be from any source she knew about.

She was aware that Alpha Force had conducted an official investigation into whether their elixir had any counterparts or competition. Their covert but thorough research had found other shifters in many U.S. locations, enough to sometimes spur legends like the one around Mary Glen, Maryland—which was why Ft. Lukman, the headquarters of Alpha Force, had been located there. The idea had been to allow normal, sane humans to ridicule those werewolf legends, and therefore add to the unit's cover.

But although quite a few shifters had apparently attempted to devise control methods, none uncovered in that ongoing research had created any viable ways to manage their shifts in any consistent and reliable manner.

They hadn't found out about Simon.

"Doing things fast would be good," Ruby said drily as she peered at Grace over her glasses. "So, like my boss here said, what's your big idea?"

"Well, though it's always possible that we'll see another outbreak of something nasty and infectious," Grace said, "we don't know when it'll happen. My suggestion is that we don't wait. We contact Major Connell, ask him to get Alpha Force to help set up a fake outbreak of something nasty, then publicize it and use all our resources to catch our bad guys."

"Not bad," Kristine said pensively. She sat closest to Grace on the no-style sofa, and Bailey lay at her feet on the worn berber carpet. "What kind of illness do you have in mind?"

"Something from a biohazard level 3," Grace said. "I'd like to have it rated, but I'd rather have it look like the cause of a disease for which a vaccination exists."

"You think our bad guys'll steal stuff that's

not especially lethal?" Autumn sounded dubious.

"People can recover from all the diseases for which they've already stolen samples," Grace reminded them. "At least so far. And that includes most types of shigellosis."

"They can," Kristine acknowledged, "but not always. A huge epidemic, if that's what they intend…well, what do you have in mind? And where would you get it from?"

"I'll just pass the idea by our fearless commanding officer. If he likes it, he can help work out the details."

But when she tried calling Drew Connell on the secure satellite phone while the gang was still around, she only got his voice mail. "Please call back as soon as you can, Major." To make sure he didn't misinterpret she added, "Nothing's wrong now, and the air-force security guys have been cooperating with me, even gave me an update. But I have something I'd like to run by you."

Grace didn't hear back from Major Connell until the first thing next morning, as she walked toward the medical center. She told him what she'd discussed with the other Alpha Force members.

"I like the idea," he said. "It would give us

better control over what's going on. What about if we staged the whole thing, brought in a group who only appeared to be sick?"

"As long as the apparent biohazard samples seem real enough, that could work," Grace said. "But we need to make it look good. What if our bad guys work in or around the hospital and are somehow involved with the testing? If it's all clearly a sham, they'll keep their distance and our efforts won't get us anywhere."

"I'll run the idea by some of the guys who are helping me work on the latest version of the elixir. Maybe take it to General Yarrow, too, for advice."

Grace knew that Drew was also a medical doctor, and he had been the first to devise the prototype elixir that allowed shifters to change at times other than the full moon and always to maintain their human cognition. Since he had helped to found Alpha Force, Drew had also called on other members who were doctors to help upgrade the formulation several times. As great as it already was, it was always subject to improvement.

She considered casually mentioning having run into another shifter here when the moon wasn't full. She probably had an obligation to do so, and if it had been anyone other than Simon she wouldn't have hesitated.

But it was Simon. She'd come up with no further ideas about how to get the truth from him, though. If her plan worked and they caught the potential terrorists, she'd either have to confront Simon for the truth…or, when she left, tell Major Connell about it. Alpha Force needed to know.

"That sounds like a good idea to me," Grace said. "General Yarrow seems to know everyone in the military, plus he has other contacts in the government. I'll bet that, with your input, he can help find the people and apparent biohazard samples we need."

"You trying to flatter both your commanding officers, Lieutenant?" Drew's voice sounded amused.

"Yes, sir," Grace said smartly. She had reached the front steps of the medical center. "How is Melanie doing?"

"She and the soon-to-be little one are getting impatient. Me, too. Otherwise, things are fine."

"Great! Well, I'm nearly on duty here now. I'll discuss the plan with you again later, if that's all right."

"Fine, Grace. Time for you to go cure some patients."

He sounded wistful, and Grace knew that despite his own medical background, Drew had been too busy to practice hands-on medicine for a while.

"I'll try to save a few for you," she said, and hung up.

That afternoon, Grace asked the nurses in the pediatric wing to bring some of the young patients to the same visitors' lounge on the second floor where Tilly had performed before. She slipped the service dog vest over her eager pup once they arrived in the area, where several children were already waiting. A couple had been there the last time, but the other three boys and a girl did not look familiar.

"Which of you is Eddie?" Grace asked. The youngster she'd have guessed was Simon's shy patient raised his hand. He had wild, longish hair and his gaze mostly settled on the floor. "This is Tilly." Grace had her dog approach the boy slowly, then sit near him. "She wants to shake hands with you."

"Really?" the boy squeaked.

"Hold out your hand and we'll see."

That was the beginning of a performance that seemed to awe the kids and delight the nursing staff observing it. Grace, too. Tilly adored the attention, and she danced and bowed and sang in a whine on command as if that was her main purpose in Alpha Force.

Grace was especially pleased to see that Simon was there as well, watching from just outside the lounge area. He caught her gaze and sent a smile in her direction, the first she'd seen from him since...well, since they'd both been doing a lot of smiling, and more, in bed together.

The memory had turned bittersweet, and Grace firmly cast it aside as she continued to give Tilly commands.

She ended the show after about twenty minutes. Both Tilly and the recuperating kids were obviously growing tired.

She still had Tilly shake hands again with each of them. When they got to Eddie, Grace said, "She really likes you and would love to tell you so if you'll ask her to speak." Although Eddie had clapped and cheered with the rest, he still seemed to favor watching the floor when Tilly was between tricks.

The child looked into Grace's face briefly. "What do I do?"

When he looked back down again, Grace said, "You'll need to look her in the eye so she'll know you're talking to her."

Slowly, Eddie raised his head and looked straight at Tilly's eyes. The dog stuck her tongue out and began to pant slightly, which caused Eddie to grin. "She looks silly."

"She's tired and a little thirsty, but she isn't going to get her drink till I tell her it's okay." Grace had put a bowl of water on the floor for the hard-working pup. It was behind a nearby chair. Of course she wouldn't keep her dog from a drink for long, but another minute or two wouldn't hurt. "First, tell her, 'Speak.'"

Eddie did so, and Tilly barked, startling the boy so he stepped back.

"That's how she speaks, honey. She can't say your name."

"I know that." Eddie looked at Grace in a manner that suggested he felt smarter than she, at least at that moment, and Grace gave him a hug.

"I know you do. Now it's time for us to go. Say goodbye, Tilly. Speak!"

Tilly barked once more, then sat still while the kids all gave her a farewell pat. The nurses, too.

As Tilly finally got her drink of water, Simon joined Grace at the side of the lounge. "That was great," he said. "I'm really pleased to see how well Eddie did. Thank you."

"You're welcome." Their gazes locked for an instant, and her insides stirred with heated memories and current desire. But reality and practicality ruled. They had to. "Are you…has anyone asked you any questions?"

"Not today," he said. "I appreciate your concern, but—"

"But you think it's unnecessary. And you're not going to tell me otherwise. I get it, Simon. Just be careful. See you around."

"I don't suppose you're having dinner in the cafeteria tonight."

She looked at him in surprise. "Is that an invitation?" She hesitated. "I'm taking Tilly over to the other wings she visited before. After that, well—I'm not sure what my plans are other than to take Tilly back to our quarters."

"If you're interested, I'll probably be there around six."

Grace was definitely interested. But she didn't know if her heart or sex drive would be able to stand another difficult session with Simon, where they remained so distant from one another. "Maybe I'll see you there," she said noncommittally.

Or not.

Only four senior citizens were in the spacious lounge where Tilly had last entertained the group instead of the six who'd been there before. All were still hospitalized and doing relatively well, the nurse in charge assured Grace when she asked. The ones not present had been scheduled for additional tests that afternoon.

Tilly didn't seem to mind having a lesser audience. Her show here once again brought attention and laughter. She took a particular liking to one of the elders in a wheelchair and kept showing off in front of him, until he chortled even louder and held out his hand, patting her on her service-dog vest.

Tilly's enhanced interest concerned Grace. She approached the patient and inhaled softly, sensing immediately what she had feared.

She approached the head nurse, drew her aside, and said, "Like a lot of dogs, Tilly's senses allow her to smell things way beyond what humans can do. The way she's hanging around that patient suggests that Tilly may smell some diseased tissue—cancerous, perhaps. If he hasn't already been checked thoroughly, I'd suggest you have it done. Or even do it again, in case it's been missed."

Grace had come in contact with many infectious diseases thanks to her medical specialty, as well as those that were not infectious. Even with her advanced senses, she seldom diagnosed a problem based solely on what she smelled. But she had often known there was a problem, like that shigellosis outbreak. And now she, too, sensed something that wasn't right. The older gentleman needed to be checked out.

"I've heard of dogs doing that," the middle-aged nurse said with her eyes wide. She smelled of disinfectant. "I'll make sure that Mr. Thomas is examined again. He's here for an injury he suffered when he fell at his military son's quarters at Zimmer, so he was probably not examined for anything besides injuries and infection."

Grace felt doubly glad to have brought Tilly to this area today. The dog who was her backup might have helped not only to enrich the lives of the people she'd entertained, but might also have saved a life. In this, Grace had been Tilly's backup.

She exited the door to the geriatric area and made sure it locked behind her, then led Tilly to the wing where patients admitted for psychiatric issues were located.

Once again, she had called ahead. The nurse in charge whom she'd met before, Ellie Yong, had acted delighted to hear from her. As a result of her call, the same PTSD patients Tilly had entertained before were in the lounge area, minus the one Grace had asked not be invited, Sgt. Norman Ivers. Several new ones were there, as well.

Pvt. Alice Johns wasted no time dashing to Tilly, kneeling and giving her a hug. One of the other two soldiers who had reacted most to Tilly before, PFC George Harper, stayed back a little, as if embarrassed at how he had embraced her before. Sgt. Jim Kubowski, who had acted indifferent until Tilly gave him her paw, required no handshake now to greet her enthusiastically.

Tilly's performance this time was brief and again got these psychologically damaged soldiers to laugh and cheer.

Grace eventually noticed that the unwelcome Sgt. Ivers had appeared after all, standing behind the crowd and watching Tilly's show with a scowl. Grace kept her eye on him. She would not let him get close to Tilly. Fortunately, he remained at a distance.

Tilly danced and rolled over and put on as good a show here as she had at their two other venues that day. When she started slowing down, clearly exhausted, Grace decided it was almost time to end the show.

Because of what had occurred with that one senior citizen, Grace first had Tilly dance around among the soldiers, just in case she sensed something inside any that required additional attention. Tilly didn't act differently toward any members of her current audience.

Grace, on the other hand, let her senses go wild—and, as she had before here, she picked up on some of the meds being used to help in the detox of these hospitalized mental patients.

She felt sorry for them. They had been to hell in their military experiences and were still recuperating. Some might never fully recuperate, and could remain addicts as well for the rest of their lives. Grace wished she could help them even more than simply having Tilly entertain them. But she knew they were being treated well at Charles Carder.

Soon, after goodbyes were said, Tilly and she headed for the locked door that would lead them back into the hospital.

Cheering up a bit once they were outside the psych wing, Grace had an urge to talk to someone about what she had experienced with Tilly. To pat her dog—and herself—on the back for possibly helping to find a previously undiagnosed disease in the elderly patient. Alpha Force members would get it. But another shifter with similar characteristics to hers, like an enhanced sense of smell in human form, would get it even more. That left out Autumn Kater, the shapeshifting hawk, despite her fascinating talents.

On her way back to her quarters with Tilly, Grace called Drew Connell. The major would definitely relate to what Grace had experienced.

He didn't answer, so Grace left a message.

Then she called Lt. Patrick Worley, who also shifted into wolf form. Patrick had recently married a nonshifter whom he'd met while on an Alpha Force mission in Alaska, an assignment in which his medical background had been irrelevant. He had investigated some really bad stuff going on around certain glaciers. He'd not only found answers, but true love, too.

Patrick answered right away. "Sorry, I can't talk right now. Alpha Force emergency. I'm on my way to the nearest base hospital—Melanie's gone into labor."

Translation: Drew's non-shifting wife was having their baby, and the doctors who worked at the military hospital where she was in labor weren't Alpha Force members. Patrick was going to help keep the unit's true nature secret, as well as to do anything to assist in the birth of Drew and Melanie's baby, which was likely to inherit his abilities. Not that they would be apparent so early. But doctors with their knowledge needed to be there in case of complications.

Which meant that neither of them would be around for a while to hold a discussion with Grace.

Not that what she had in mind was urgent. She didn't really need a pat on the back. Even so, she felt a sense of isolation. Sure, she could get together with fellow Alpha Force members here, but none would fully get it.

That was when she realized she was just giving herself excuses. There was someone else here she could talk to. In fact, a substantial part of her mood was undoubtedly the result of wanting to talk with him.

Not that she could really tell him what she had experienced, and why.

But seeing Simon just might make her feel less alone.

Chapter 10

This was a bad idea, Grace thought a short while later.

She had shown up at the hospital cafeteria at the time Simon had said he would be there and bought a steak sandwich to satisfy her canine appetite, along with a small salad for her health-conscious human side.

He was already sitting in the area where they had dined previously, munching on a hamburger.

He stood quickly when he saw her and took her tray. His hand brushed hers momentarily before he placed her food on the table. The pleased expression on his great-looking face nearly took her breath away. "Glad you made it, Grace," he said. "One of these days, though, we'll have to try a real restaurant."

"One that doesn't pass along shigellosis."

"Sounds good to me."

Grace took a seat across from him. As always, the cafeteria was crowded, both with staff and visitors. No one near them sat alone, so there was some degree of privacy for their conversation.

Even so, Grace knew the moment she sat down what a mistake this was. Judging by the way he regarded her with sexy, suggestive eyes, he had the wrong idea about why she had joined him. Sort of wrong, anyway.

She wasn't about to engage with him in hot, mindless sex tonight. Even though, despite all her qualms, the idea ignited her insides, made her wish things were different.

Made her body beg for her mind to toss away all rational thought.

But she had come here for a sense of camaraderie with a fellow shifter. Even so, she couldn't possibly have that with Simon. There were too many complications. She didn't even dare to hint now that they had such a background in common.

She grasped for a neutral topic, finally deciding on Tilly. But it didn't stay neutral.

"I'm not sure, but I think she might have sensed some disease in a geriatric patient who came to watch her. He was an accident victim and had apparently undergone no tests for cancer or anything else, but Tilly seemed to catch some underlying smell." So had Grace, but she wasn't about to mention that.

"It'll be interesting to see if the tests reveal anything."

"Sure will. I know of dogs trained to scent diseases. I've sometimes thought—well, certain people might have that capability, too." Like shapeshifters, at least those who didn't rein in their abilities out of self-preservation.

"No kidding," he said. "Interesting possibility, but I don't know of anything like that."

He was lying, or at least edging around the truth. He surely smelled disease as much as she did, working in a hospital.

She considered asking him obliquely about what he did pick up around here, scents or sounds that normal but alert nonshifters might also become aware of, but decided against it. She'd already gone about as far as she dared—for now—on that subject.

When they were done eating, Simon looked at her. "Are we friends again?"

She knew what he was asking. Everything

inside her wanted to shout a gleeful yes…everything but her mind.

"I don't think we're arguing right now, so, yes, we're friends. But not friends with benefits, if that's what you're asking."

"Not now, maybe. But I'm hoping to change that again, Grace. I think you enjoyed the other night as much as I did."

"The sexy part, yes," she agreed, smiling at him. "But you hated the rest even more than I did. Anyway, it's been nice eating with you again. See you tomorrow."

Ignoring her regret, she left to return to her apartment.

To Grace's surprise, Drew Connell did call her back that night. "How's Melanie?" she asked right away.

"We're now the proud parents of a beautiful little girl. Emily. She's bound to be a shifter like her dad, and her mom says she's thrilled about it."

"Congratulations to all of you!"

"Now tell me what you wanted to discuss."

It seemed a little anticlimactic after his news, but Grace told him about Tilly and her possible scenting of illness in a patient.

"Did you try to confirm it with your own senses, Grace?" Drew's voice was wry.

"Yes, and she was right. I smelled a scent of illness, too, when I approached the man. It's interesting how many smells there are in a hospital setting—cleaners, the meds and narcotics used by the PTSD patients, the odor of the shigellosis epidemic…"

"You were warned to control your canine senses as much as possible there, Grace. Those of us who're doctors mostly work in small practices, or in labs like we do at Alpha Force. The additional smells and sounds can be pretty overwhelming if you let them."

"I know. But I'm still a doctor as well as an Alpha Force operative. I intend to help people."

"That's fine, as long as you don't do it at the expense of our mission—or yourself."

A long while after dinner with Grace, Simon returned downstairs to the lab he had virtually commandeered as his own—not that anyone had officially approved of it. Or even really knew about it.

When there earlier that evening, he had hidden the pills he was working on, as always, more or less in plain sight. Now, he unlocked the deep drawer among the many cabinets in this room that comprised its elongated lab stations. Wearing disposable latex gloves and a sanitary lab jacket, he pulled the bottles containing his special pills from among the preparations he did discuss with others— the homeopathic healing formulations he was working on to help his infectious-disease patients regain their strength.

His shifting formula had worked well that evening, but not perfectly. As usual, he had felt light-headed after changing back to human form. Consequently, he still hadn't reached the degree of success he sought, and with all that had occurred on the night of his last shift he had not had much opportunity to return here and work on it.

Maybe he should thank Grace for declining his invitation for another night of nonstop sex. He snorted to himself. No, thanking her for that wasn't on his agenda. No matter how eager he was to get his pills to work perfectly, a delay to accommodate making love with Grace would be worth it.

The smell here of antiseptic solutions used to clean the counters frequently, as well as the gleaming gray-patterned linoleum floor, was nearly overwhelming, as always. He figured that even people without an improved sense of smell would find it miserable. But he accepted its necessity.

Now Simon booted up the mini notebook computer he had brought along and typed in his password. The way he entered data about his supplements and other creations, no one but he could interpret them anyway, but he took no chances. He had already determined what tweaks he would perform to his shifting formulation but wanted to double-check it before he gave it a try.

What would Grace think if she knew what he was really doing here?

Why had she stopped teasing him about whether he could be a werewolf? Had she been serious the other day in her extreme hinting that she now knew he was one?

He hoped not. He might be damned attracted to her, but her knowing for certain what he was could only cause a lot of complications.

He suddenly stopped typing as some of what Grace had said before carved a curious thought into his brain, one that nagged at him. She had indicated that Tilly, trained as a service dog to entertain hospital patients, might have smelled something more serious in an accident patient. She had suggested that certain people might have the same abilities. Was this a prod at him, more subtle than in the old days, suggesting that shapeshifters might have that ability?

Simon did, in fact, often sense previously undiagnosed diseases in hospital patients. He then had to find a way to discreetly ensure that the patient underwent appropriate testing.

He was almost always correct.

Did Grace have that ability? The fact that she no longer hinted that she might be a shifter made him more suspicious that she was one.

Not that it mattered. Not really. He had too much to hide from her to play games with her, no matter what rules she seemed to be imposing these days.

"Too bad, Grace," he muttered aloud. He would love to believe they'd get together again soon, and often, for sex.

But for his self-preservation, even if she suddenly became interested again, that wasn't going to happen.

"Dr. Andreas? This is Lotty Gail. I'm the head nurse on duty at the Charles Carder E.R. tonight."

Grace was in bed at her quarters on the airforce base. She had been lying there for what felt like hours, her mind too keyed up to allow her to sleep. "Yes, Lotty?"

"Sorry to bother you so late when you're not on call, but we've got some emergency cases that just came in. We're drawing blood for tests, but the problem seems to be some kind of infection. There are four patients, and all we have here at the moment is one resident. Could you—"

"I'll be there in fifteen minutes."

Simon received the call on his cell phone while he was finally walking home to his apartment that night. He turned back toward the hospital immediately.

As he reached the door to the E.R., he saw Grace approaching through the parking lot. "Do you know what's happening?" she asked.

"Only that there's some kind of outbreak." He held the door open for her, and she hurried in, her silver-blond hair shining beneath the artificial hospital lights. Her determination and dedication appealed to him. Hell, everything about her appealed to him—when their topics of conversation didn't hint of shapeshifting.

Lotty Gail, the nurse in charge that night, rushed toward them, looking harried. She was a small, middle-aged woman with whom Simon had worked in the E.R. before. She always seemed a little nervous, but her competence was unwavering.

"You're the doctors and have to make the final diagnosis," she said, "but the patients are all in one family that went camping and came back with this. They have rashes and other symptoms that look to me like the outbreak of

Rocky Mountain spotted fever back in 2004. The mother did say she was grossed out when they found ticks in their sleeping bags."

"Sounds possible," Grace said, and Simon agreed.

They both went immediately to the clean room, where they donned sterile clothing, disposable gloves and face masks. Then they divided up who would see which patients. Simon got the father and older son, and Grace got the mother and younger son.

The E.R. resident was in the cubicle with the father when Simon arrived. While keeping up cheerful banter with the patient, the resident conveyed to Simon what tests he'd taken and the man's vital signs, and Simon checked the chart that had been started.

He then went to consult with Grace. The nurse's preliminary diagnosis appeared potentially correct. They would not wait until test results were back, but would begin treating these patients with appropriate antibiotics immediately.

Simon couldn't help wondering what would happen to the blood and other fluid samples taken from the patients after they were tested. Would they become yet another target for the thieves?

Rocky Mountain spotted fever might not

present as much of a risk as an extreme strain of shigellosis as the basis for a biological weapon, since it could be treated more easily. But that hadn't stopped the thieves before. The fact that it was passed along by ticks might stop them, though—if the thieves knew that.

In any event, the disease rated a biohazard level 3, so that might make it attractive to whomever was stealing samples here.

Simon was glad he'd had even a brief opportunity before to work on his own pills. A secretive wolf just might be the most appropriate observer of the storage building if the samples were again taken there before incineration.

"Yes, sir," Grace said to Major Drew Connell over their secure satellite phone. She had him on the speaker.

It was early morning, and she was back in her quarters with Tilly—along with the rest of the Alpha Force contingent at Zimmer Air Force Base. They'd had to pull Autumn in. She had been on duty under her cover assignment of being a communications officer.

"We know the risk of these materials getting stolen," she continued. "Our thieves might feel drunk with power that they've gotten away with it so many times."

"It'd be a good thing if you could catch them

this time, before we get our alternate plan in order and send a bunch of military guys who'll play sick. As much as I like the concept, it might be a problem keeping it secret there."

The others had all congratulated Drew already on becoming a father. Then they'd discussed the importance of keeping all their operations completely under wraps. Grace had not been able to cross off any of the people in charge from her suspect list. That included the guy who'd grumpily called them for help in the first place, Colonel Nelson Otis, and the chief medical officer in charge of the Infectious Diseases Center, Captain Moe Scoles. And definitely the head security officer, Major Louis Dryson.

So far, Grace had not been able to account for Captain Scoles's whereabouts last night. Not that his absence made him more of a suspect. But it didn't make him any less of one, either.

"Acknowledged, sir," Grace said. She looked first at Autumn, then at Kristine and Ruby. "If these guys dare to try to steal the biohazards this time, we're going to get them."

Chapter 11

Two days had passed. The Rocky Mountain spotted fever patients remained in the hospital, kept in a small isolation unit near the E.R. that had separately enclosed rooms for each one. The patients were recuperating and were expected to be released soon.

Which pleased Grace.

Plus, the senior patient whom Tilly had singled out—and who'd also emitted a scent of disease to Grace—had been diagnosed with a fortunately treatable form of cancer.

Now Grace sat at her computer in her small hospital office, going over the records of the Rocky Mountain spotted fever patients that had been entered into the system. She had continued to help treat them after the diagnosis was confirmed.

So had Simon. She had seen a lot of him over the past couple of days—all business. Mostly formal.

If she didn't count the smoldering glances he sometimes aimed in her direction. Ones she attempted to return cordially yet coolly.

Even so, she knew she couldn't always keep her desire for him out of her expression. After greeting him she always walked away.

Her cell phone beeped, signaling a text message.

It was from Kristine and said simply: Samples to be taken to storage tonight.

Grace stood with Kristine in the shadows at the far side of the parking lot near the storage and incineration building. Both wore dark clothing, and Kristine toted her ever-present backpack. Among its contents was Grace's military firearm, but she would soon not be in a form to avail herself of it. She hoped that a weapon like that would not be needed.

"Flirting with the security staff has its advantages," Kristine whispered, then grinned.

"I suspected that was how you got your information." Grace kept her voice low, too.

There were a lot of cars around, few people, but with the security cameras as sensitive as they were, she didn't want what they said to come out in an intelligible recording. "Did they tell you the time, who would bring it and what security measures were being taken?"

"I didn't get into details like that, for obvious reasons. But the guy was cute—and knew it. When I played the scared little sexpot who worried about whether the latest nasty stuff might get stolen again, he assured me that all would be taken care of. The stuff wouldn't even be stored, just incinerated right away. He even laughingly admitted to having caused some confusion recently when some samples were stolen. He and his buddies had ordered pizza. They sent the delivery guy, a friend, out to stock a party they'd intended to go to later with some special beer they kept here for a special occasion. They later had to clear the friend from being a suspect. Also, the whole situation didn't seem funny at the time, since he and his buddies were knocked out while on duty—but he wouldn't let that happen again. He was alert, not fooling around. He'd keep me safe."

"Interesting," Grace said. "And pretty much as we'd suspected." She paused. "So, sexpot, did you arrange to see him again?"

"I told him my big, hulking pilot boyfriend would be back tonight, darn it all."

Grace laughed. "Ever thought of taking up acting?"

Kristine raised her black eyebrows. "A lot of what I do is acting, boss. Covering for you takes talent."

"Amen."

The samples currently being brought to the storage building did not contain the same level of contagion as those that had been stolen before, since RMSF was transmitted by vectors—parasites—in this case ticks. Even so, since the motive for the thefts was as unknown as the identities of the thieves, another incident was definitely possible.

Grace wished there was some way of hiding in the tunnel and following whoever took charge of moving the samples. Better yet, shadow the samples themselves. But her presence in either form would be obvious. Instead, she again chose to observe from the parking lot.

"There." Kristine pointed toward the concrete storage shed. From the direction of the tunnel exit, two men in sterile clothing emerged carrying a large cylinder, followed by others in camo uniforms holding their weapons ready. The door to the office where the security guys were posted opened, then shut quickly again behind the men carrying, and guarding, the biohazards.

"Appears like it's time for me to get busy." Grace looked up first toward the palm tree nearest the building. A lone hawk perched on top of one of the lower branches. The tall tree swayed gently in the light, hot breeze, and so did its dangling limbs, but the hawk appeared steady and unfazed. "Between Autumn and me, maybe we'll catch the bad guys tonight."

"Let's hope so. Come on. We need to go."

They hurried to the location they had chosen for its seclusion, the same one they had used before along the border of the hospital property and the air-force base. There, hidden by the hedges, Grace stripped while Kristine pulled out the Alpha Force elixir and got the light ready. Grace downed the potion and waited.

In moments, with the light shining on her, she felt the beginning of her shift. Her limbs tightened, her insides moved, and the familiar stretching and discomfort took over.

"Be careful," she heard Kristine call softly— the last impression she had before her human form was gone.

The feel of sand, then concrete beneath her feet meant freedom.

Leaving the strong, choking fuel smell be-

hind, she loped joyously, cautiously, back to where she had last been. She inhaled deeply once more. There was a different fuel smell here. Gasoline, among the cars.

How close did she dare go? The security cameras might be operating fully this night. Plus, many guards and others would be on high alert.

She paced behind the autos, continuing to move her ears, listening. Staying far from people parking and exiting their cars, or entering them and driving off.

She identified the talk of those within the building. Heard no voices outside it. No footsteps.

No smells of other people walking around it—or was there one? On the other side?

It resembled Simon's scent. Was that wishful thinking on her part...or fear? That he was in fact the thief? Or was the fear for him?

Cautiously, she prowled closer. Scented the hawk still in the tree. Observed, with all her senses, the building that remained her focus.

Watched the guards who stood on the paved area outside the structure. They appeared alert, but not distressed.

The outside door to the office opened. The men in protective clothing walked out, then into the incineration unit. After they emerged, the smell of heat and ignition fuel followed them.

No incident tonight?

That was good.

It was also bad. Had the thieves seen the extra security and backed off for now?

She no longer believed it was Simon, but his probable presence tonight taunted her. Maybe she had been right in suspecting him.

Or maybe he was protecting himself by trying, also, to catch the thieves.

She had wanted—intended—to catch the thieves, whoever they were. That would not happen this night.

But she had no doubt that they would act again.

Simon stayed far from the storage building. A lot of security was present tonight. He wasn't sure exactly what had gone down, but when the guys in moon suits left, heading back with the armed guys in uniform toward the tunnel entrance, he figured it was over, and nothing had gone wrong.

This time.

No one could accuse him of anything—not even Grace. He hadn't even shifted, planning to only if he saw anything suspicious.

But with all the other scents around here,

he'd thought he had gotten a hint of another wolf's.

There had been activity in the parking lot, too. Visitors arriving and leaving. A few people walking around, although none had approached the storage and incineration building except for the guys in charge of the biohazards—or so he believed.

The warm breeze picked up a little as he decided it was time to leave. He had been standing behind a large SUV that concealed him from view of anyone in the building and its cameras, and this area was far enough from the hospital entrances that no one around there would have noticed him either.

A movement startled him—a shadow. A large bird had just flown beneath one of the parking-lot lights. A hawk? It circled majestically overhead. He watched it for a long minute until it flew in the direction of the air-force base.

Which was when he saw something moving between some of the farthest cars beneath where the bird had just flown.

An animal? It disappeared again behind a car. Could it be the wolf he thought he had scented? Most likely it was just a dog that belonged to a visitor, one that had been released outside to do its duty.

But maybe not. It wouldn't hurt to find out.

Wolves might exist around here. Real ones. And others like him?

What if—?

It could be Grace—or not. When she had hinted about being a shapeshifter years ago, he had assumed she was baiting a trap for him like those cursed nonshifters who had harmed his family.

Now that they were reunited—sort of—she had acted as if she knew *he* was a shifter but had no longer hinted that she could be one, too.

He needed to find out.

He wasn't able to get closer yet, though. He needed to keep his speed similar to that of the creature he followed so he didn't spook it. If it was a dog, no harm, no foul. If it was a wolf, even a shifter, it would be able to smell him even better than he could smell it.

Unless—he looked up toward the palm trees above. Determined the way the breeze blew.

Made sure he stayed upwind of the creature as he continued in the direction he believed it was heading. *She* was heading.

He would find out for sure, but he felt almost certain it was Grace.

Glimpses of fur between vehicles, then along the hedges between the two properties, kept him going. If she could not smell him, he was in a similar position of not being able to scent her, especially in human form with his senses so limited.

And then… Damn it. He'd lost her. He no longer saw or otherwise sensed her.

Even so, he kept going in the direction she seemed to have been heading, along the thick hedges that separated the hospital from the adjoining base. He had to be even more careful now. He didn't want to be surprised by catching up with her. Or going farther than she had so she ran into him.

He walked slowly, cautiously, trying to make no noise on the sandy path, raising his head to scent the air the best he could in his nonwolf form.

Then he heard a voice. Low, urgent, soothing. Grace's? No, it didn't sound like her. Whose, then? Someone talking to the creature—the wolf? Grace?

He edged in the direction of the whisper. Moved upwind of it again, and stayed in the cover of the tall hedges as best he could.

There. Looking through a slight opening in the branches with their green but browning leaves, he saw someone. A person, not a canine. It was that nurse who was new to the hospital, who had arrived at the same time Grace did and appeared to be her aide. What was her name? Sgt. Norwood. Kristine.

She was looking down, and Simon maneuvered to see what she was staring at.

A wolf. He wasn't surprised. But it wasn't only a wolf. It was a shifter, starting the metamorphosis he mostly experienced himself and hadn't observed for a long time, since moving away from his family.

Mesmerized, he continued to watch through the branches that were his cover but that also kept him from having as good a view as he craved.

Nevertheless, he saw the wolfen body twisting. Gyrating. Absorbing the fur that was its silvery pelt, even as it was replaced by smooth, human skin.

And when the transformation was complete, it proffered the view he had anticipated all along. Only for a moment, though, since Kristine Norwood had come prepared with clothing, which she held out toward the woman who stood there.

The gorgeous woman with the body that made Simon's own react immediately, despite the unusual circumstances.

Grace.

Simon watched from where he stood for as long as Grace and Kristine remained where they were.

He knew what it was like to need to catch

one's breath after a shift. To wait until the feelings of stretching and aching finally dissipated. To shake off the feeling of light-headedness.

He couldn't always remain where he had been during a shift to let those sensations ebb and disappear. Probably Grace couldn't, either. Not all the time.

But everything around them was quiet for now. They didn't need to move quickly.

When they finally did, he followed them. Quietly, staying as far back as he could without losing them.

He knew now that Grace was able to sense him, scent him, as easily as he could use his special perceptive abilities to detect her location. If he remained distant, she wouldn't necessarily pay attention to any sign that another shifter was about. Maybe.

She hadn't acted aware of him so far, a good thing.

In fact, the two women did not act particularly wary or even vigilant as they began walking from the area obscured by the hedges. Maybe they felt a sense of security after observing that the apparent object of their scrutiny tonight, the biohazard samples, had been dealt with appropriately and were not stolen this time.

Both, despite the heat, wore black long-sleeved shirts and jeans, most likely to aid in their avoiding detection earlier. Now they strode along the air-force base pathways between sand-strewn areas of sparse vegetation. Fortunately, or perhaps not fortunately, there were hangars and sheds along the way. The structures obscured him but also made it more difficult to follow by watching.

His senses of smell and hearing led him in the right direction, though. There was always Grace's floral scent, muted now since he didn't dare get close. Plus, the two women were talking in soft-enough tones that he could not make out what was said.

Of course ordinary people would not be able to hear even that.

Why was he following? He wasn't exactly sure. Maybe to confirm where Grace lived.

Maybe, if Kristine ever left her company, he could hurry ahead and confront Grace and...

Then what?

No, he needed to think this through first.

It was a good idea for him to learn where to find her.

It was a bad idea for him to rush into any action. He would probably regret anything he did. Especially if he did it rashly.

But Grace Andreas was a shapeshifter like

him, as he had somewhat suspected from shortly after they had met so long ago.

They eventually entered a building on the outskirts of the airfield. Grace must have an apartment there. Presumably, her dog—Tilly—waited for her there.

Should he wait a few minutes to give her time to get in, then call?

Or… If Tilly had been inside all this time, Grace would need to take her for a walk. That might be a good time for Simon to confront her. As long as he'd decided on the best approach by then.

He was right, he discovered about ten minutes later. Only he had been only partially correct. Grace had Tilly out for a walk, but Kristine, with another dog, was with her.

Just as well. The prudent thing for him to do would be to sleep on this situation.

He'd know his approach by tomorrow.

Chapter 12

Grace was irritated. In her standard medical garb, she strode along the third floor hallway of Charles Carder, from the office where its commanding officer, Colonel Nelson Otis, and Major Louis Dryson, commanding officer of the Air Force Security Forces stationed at Zimmer, had confronted her.

It was the morning after the biohazard incineration with the happy ending. Nothing stolen. No one gassed or otherwise hurt.

But also no indication of who the thieves were. She had no doubt they would strike again if the occasion presented itself—like another round of more dangerous substances being collected.

The colonel and major had called her to meet with them first thing on her arrival that day. Then, together, they had taken credit for how well things had gone the night before.

That wasn't so bad. Grace was sure that no one in Alpha Force gave a damn about who took credit for a success, even if some of the special-ops members had been involved—and last night, they'd only been observers. Plus, the unit wouldn't publicly pat itself on the back for a triumph anyway.

If the combined determination of the chief medical officer at the hospital and the security force at the air-force base was that they were masters of the situation, fine.

No matter that they hadn't actually achieved anything.

The operation had been a success primarily because there was no situation that needed to be countered. No one had attempted to steal the fluid samples.

Could it have been because of the extra security that had been so obvious? Maybe the thieves, knowing of the extra precautions and concern, had decided to back off…for now.

Or maybe it had been because of the nature of the Rocky Mountain spotted fever samples, and the fact that the tick-transmitted disease was less likely to become a terrorist weapon.

After hurrying down a flight of steps and along another couple of hallways, Grace reached the Infectious Diseases Center. She entered the small office that was hers as long as she was there.

That was the crux of it. The two senior officers, while patting themselves on the back, also determined that their quasi-combat situation was resolved. They had handled it just fine this time, and could handle it in the future.

They no longer needed the secretive special-ops unit Alpha Force to watch their backs. Or so they said.

They had no idea of how their backs had been watched last night, by a hawk overhead and a keen-sensed wolf on the ground, ready to follow terrorists or anyone else who might have attempted to steal the targeted materials.

Were the thefts over? Grace doubted it. Could the security forces here deal with any attempts, as the colonel and major had professed?

Maybe. But if they failed, and something else as potentially lethal as the highly dangerous strain of shigellosis samples were taken, it would be a matter of national security way beyond what they could deal with here.

Colonel Otis had said he had notified Drew Connell about the moving of the hazardous substances last night, as he had before. Now the major needed to know about this latest confrontation as quickly as possible.

Soon, sitting behind her small desk, Grace punched the button on her cell phone to call Drew. The special, secure satellite phone was in her apartment, so she would have to be discreet in what she said.

She got Drew's voice mail. Not surprising. The guy had just become a father. Yes, he'd be interested in hearing this—but it clearly wasn't the top priority on his agenda for now. She left a message telling him that things could be in flux here and that she needed to talk to him ASAP.

She checked her watch. She was now officially on duty at the hospital, so she stuffed her phone into her pocket, locked her purse in her desk, and prepared to head for the rooms of the Infectious Diseases Center to start assisting with patients.

As she opened her door, she nearly walked right into Simon. She gasped as he grabbed her arms to steady her. "You startled me," she stammered. "What are you doing here?"

"We need to talk, Grace. I spent all night considering my options about how to start this conversation, and decided that just doing it spontaneously would be best. But not here." The scowl on the face she had come to know so well sent a current of unease sparking up her spine along with the usual tingling of sexual interest. What was this about?

Was he finally about to admit who, and what, he was? If so, why now?

Or was that just wishful thinking on her part?

"All right." She kept her tone even despite the continuing pulsation of emotions within her. "I'm not sure how much time I'll have. I'm on duty. Are you?"

"Yes, but this can't wait." The dark gold of his eyes seemed to radiate a warning. Of what? She must be imagining it. "I stopped at the main desk in the department on my way here. There are no current infectious-disease emergencies, fortunately, and Moe Scoles is in his office. He'll contact us if that changes. For now, we can check in on patients a little late." He paused and moved back, finally releasing her. She regretted the sudden loss of contact, knew that her reaction was absurd—especially considering his apparently distressed mood. "Let's go take a walk."

"As long as it's not outside." Though it was

still morning, the soaring desert heat promised
to bake anyone unsheltered within its intensity.

"We'll stay in the lobby."

Where there were always lots of folks who'd
all be thinking about why they were at the hospital that day—to see patients, to work, to talk
to a doctor, whatever. None would pay attention to two people off in a corner.

Grace assumed Simon wanted to avoid the
possibility of someone eavesdropping on their
conversation. Fine with her. Her intention
wasn't to let the rest of the ordinary world know
that there were truly such things as shapeshifters.

She only wanted Simon to, at last, admit to
her he was one.

Once he did, she would have to come up
with a tactful way to ask how he could change
outside a full moon. Then, somehow, get him
to share whatever breakthrough was allowing
him to do it.

Maybe then she would dare to admit she was
one, too, without hinting of the true nature of
Alpha Force. Confessing to her abilities might
make the entire unit seem suspect, but maybe
she could come up with a feasible story about
how she blended in without anyone knowing
who she really was.

As they walked along the corridor toward

the stairs of the second floor entry, Grace was highly aware of Simon's tall presence beside her. He began to stride faster, so she accommodated him. Why was he in such a hurry?

"Here," he said when they reached the visitors area on that floor, where Tilly had entertained children the couple of times Grace brought her. "This should be quiet enough."

The small lounge was unoccupied. Grace glanced up and saw the security cameras, but Simon must have seen them, too. He moved a couple of the upholstered chairs around so their backs would be all that could get photographed. In case the equipment also recorded sound, Grace knew that Simon and she would need to speak softly.

As they sat, Simon said, "I should have brought us some coffee, or even water. We could go to the cafeteria, but staying there probably wouldn't be a good idea."

Grace translated. She might talk to Simon about things that they wouldn't want public. Late morning in the cafeteria, before a lunch crowd arrived, would be a bad time for that. People could be there individually on their breaks. Whatever. They could listen in more easily to things that didn't concern them—but were of critical importance to Grace and to Simon.

"I'm fine," Grace assured him. She sat on one of the chairs as he did the same, then waited. This was his show.

He leaned down toward her so their heads almost touched. Why did something like that seem so sensual to her? Maybe his very presence was enough to start her hormones simmering. But she needed to get them under control. Even if she decided to sleep with him again—which she wouldn't—this wasn't the place to even consider it.

His deep voice was soft and husky. "I saw you last night, Grace."

She drew in her breath so fast that she nearly coughed. That wasn't what she had anticipated.

It couldn't mean what she initially assumed...could it?

"That's interesting," she replied noncommittally. "Not surprising since I work here, too, though. Why didn't you say hi?" She purposely acted dense and cool, tamping down the initial panic that had raced through her.

"I saw you *change,* Grace."

Her heart slammed as if it had suddenly regenerated into a jackhammer.

A couple of nurses walked by and glanced toward them, mild curiosity in their gazes as they continued talking about the hot Phoenix-area weather. They smelled of the ubiquitous hospital disinfectant.

Grace felt as if the world was eavesdropping, but she knew not even those nearby people could hear her conversation with Simon.

"I—I don't understand," she finally responded softly. That was a lie. She knew what he was talking about. But she couldn't admit anything without letting her mind churn around it and decide how to handle this catastrophic situation.

"Yes, you do. You know exactly what I mean. I was in the parking lot, too, around the storage building. Even though I have nothing to do with security for the biohazards, I've been damned concerned about how they've been handled. The thefts. Whether the stuff has gotten into the worst hands possible. It's bad enough being an infectious-diseases specialist when even a small epidemic occurs naturally. But the idea of having to try to save hundreds of lives. Thousands. All because samples that should have been incinerated were, instead, stolen... Well, I at least had to observe. Plus, I know I was a suspect last time, so watching was also a form of self-preservation."

Grace latched on to that as her own form of self-preservation. "You're sure you weren't there to cover your butt?" she accused, purposely not even glancing toward that firm, sexy part of his body. "You'd have been better off if someone else saw you and could vouch for your noninvolvement if this batch was taken, too."

Maybe she could turn the tables on him. Fast. Put him on the defensive instead of her.

"Could be," he said, "but it wasn't taken. Plus, there aren't many people I'd trust to watch my back, and the primary one—you—were obviously preoccupied." How could he both attack her and make her feel all gooey inside at the same time? He trusted her? Then why were they having this conversation instead of the one she'd hoped for?

"You didn't ask," she said, as if that would have made all the difference in the world. Maybe it would have.

"No," he replied. "I didn't. I decided to handle things differently, right or wrong. It turned out to be right, in several ways."

The angles of his face seemed suddenly sharper as he stared at her, but—was that a hint of compassion she saw in his eyes? Why?

"Last night I sensed a canine presence, Grace," he continued, "and not for the first time. When it seemed clear that the extracted fluids had been successfully incinerated, I figured it was time to leave the area. I'd hung out there with the excuse, if anyone asked, of wanting to assure myself that all was handled correctly. Fortunately, no one seemed to be patrolling the farthest areas of the parking lot. No one except…well, an animal that smelled like, and appeared to be, a wolf."

She paid attention to what he said. It was far from an admission that he, too, was a shifter, but at least suggested advanced senses.

"There are feral wolves in this area." Her acknowledgment wasn't an admission that she was one of them.

His smile—why was it so sexy, when what he said was so threatening? It was warm and amused…and unnerving. "I know that as much as you do. I followed this one. It—she—met a human being we both know, Kristine Norwood. I know she's a friend of yours, a nurse who's attached to the same military unit. You both arrived here the same time. Anyway…Grace, I saw you shift."

What a damned inconvenient time for her cell phone to ring. She grabbed at her pocket. Should she let it go? Answer it?

What if it was the major returning her call? She couldn't exactly talk to him now.

But maybe the distraction was perfect. She had no idea, yet, how to respond to Simon. Other than— "Wait just a minute, Simon, while I take this call. Oh, and by the way, I saw you shifting a few nights ago. I hinted at it, sure— but I was mostly waiting for you to admit it at last."

Simon laughed aloud while Grace held her phone as tightly as a lifeline, skirted a few people strolling along, and fled to the far side of the lounge area.

She'd seen him, too? How ironic was that?

But why had she pushed him to admit it without disclosing her actual knowledge?

Because she knew he'd ask if she was a shapeshifter too, and she didn't want to admit it?

She hadn't exactly hinted at it recently. Had something changed since they'd been together years ago? Or had she simply decided not to even bring it up unless he did? Or until she actually saw him change.

He watched her now. There was something surreptitious in the way she guarded her phone as she spoke into it. Who was on the other end? What was she saying?

He listened, but of course she knew of his acuity of hearing, just as he knew of hers. He could hear her speaking, but her tone was much too muted for him to make out her words.

He watched, though. And waited. He glanced at his watch. He really would need to get back to the infectious-diseases area soon and start checking on his patients.

But for right now, he'd exercise patience instead...and wait a little longer to find out what Grace would say to him next.

Grace felt as if she was performing a juggling act. Not entertaining kids or others undergoing treatment at the hospital like Tilly did, but verbally, and with her mind.

"Yes, sir," she said to Major Drew Connell. As she had suspected, he had returned her call at this inconvenient time. "But despite everything going well last night, with nothing stolen and the samples incinerated right away, we can't be sure nothing will happen next time."

And okay, not everything went well last night. But just as she hadn't told her commanding officer that she had seen the man who had once been, and was again, her lover shapeshifting, and outside of a full moon at that, she didn't want to mention that he had seen her as well. She needed to get a better grasp on the possible scenarios that this could generate.

None of them, to her initially distressed mind, could be good.

"I agree, Grace." Drew had already responded to her platitudes and questions about his new baby daughter. Now they were on business—and what needed to happen next. "I liked your idea of taking a proactive approach. Especially since, you said, the powers that be want to oust Alpha Force soon. I'll have General Yarrow call and fix that, at least for a while. Meantime, I want to talk to you about how best to send in a team of 'sick' folks to get this done, but now isn't a good time."

For her either, but she didn't want to tell him that. "Let's schedule a conference call soon," she said. "Sometime when I'm not at the hospital. I'm being cautious, of course." Like keeping her voice so low that Simon shouldn't be able to eavesdrop—she hoped. "But with all the security here, I'm not entirely comfortable about speaking freely."

"Got it. I'd also like General Yarrow's participation, if he can make it work. He'll want some input."

"Great. Why don't you check with him, I'll check with my fellow Alpha Forcers here, and we'll coordinate a good time."

"Fine. Meantime, Grace… I can tell you're

being cautious, since I can barely hear you. But just be careful. There are still a lot of things that can go wrong."

She turned slightly to glance at Simon. He was still there, watching her. "I know, sir," she said.

Chapter 13

Despite his smugness, Simon felt wary as Grace returned to the chair she had vacated in the lounge. She didn't sit but looked down at him.

"I've got to get to work," she said, without mentioning her phone call. Not that he was surprised. But he was curious. "I don't think this conversation is over, though. Why don't we plan on having dinner together this evening? Not here. Let's try to come up with someplace where we can talk—without being overheard."

"Fine." He kept his tone casual, but inside he felt a rush of triumph. Why? He wasn't sure, especially since their next conversation was likely to be tense.

Like him, she was a medical doctor. Now he knew that wasn't all she shared with him.

He'd wondered about nurse Kristine Norwood. He'd checked, and she was a sergeant in the military, in the same unit as Grace, one called Alpha Force.

Kristine knew what Grace was. Her assistance included helping when Grace shifted.

How did that work? Did other members of their unit know?

He'd have to ask Grace, as well as extract information from her about how she was able to shift last night, so far from a full moon. But now wasn't the time to pursue any of that.

He was acutely aware of her presence as they both walked the halls toward the Infectious Diseases Center. She strode so fast that he increased his own pace to high gear, too.

When they arrived, she looked up at him. There was a chill on her lovely face that made him regret—almost—his revelation to her. "I trust you won't mention our conversation and your…allegations to anyone. No one would believe you anyway."

He couldn't help a brief, rueful smile. "I'm well aware of that, Grace." Even though she'd told him she had seen him shift, that was as close to an admission from Grace about her abilities as he'd gotten so far. "Let's talk sometime this afternoon about where to have dinner."

A respite from talking with Simon had both good and bad points, Grace thought as she returned to her office. She'd have time to digest what he'd said, to figure out how to handle things in their next discussions.

That also meant she would think about little else for now, and probably for a long time—if she let herself.

But she was a doctor, on staff here not only to work undercover but also to help patients. For the moment, at least, she wouldn't focus on Simon or what he knew or their impending conversation tonight.

She checked the computer for updates on patients assigned to her, then got to work, concentrating on their needs, using her usual caring bedside manner with each.

Between rooms, she let herself think briefly of Simon. Couldn't help it, since she glimpsed him often.

He stayed away from her, but at times she wanted to smack the sexy, ironic grin from his face as he nodded in greeting. Instead, she smiled back grimly, as if she considered him out of line.

It almost felt, at times, as if they were the only ones in the hallways. Not true, of course. Nurses passed briskly by while doing their jobs. Visitors came to see patients whose contagious stages had passed. Orderlies and other doctors and staff…

And Simon.

The first time Kristine approached, it was clear that her aide knew something was up. "You okay, Grace?" she asked in a low voice as Grace prepared to enter another patient's room. Today, she wore an aqua nurse's uniform. "Every time I've seen you today you look— well, almost zombie-like. Going about your business without noticing me or anyone else. What's up?"

Grace made herself smile. Shoving her fists into the pockets of her white lab jacket, she looked into her assistant's blue eyes and raised her chin like Kristine's.

"I'm just tired," she said. "And concerned. We really need to have that conversation with Major Connell about how to…incite the kind of incident we're here to deal with." That should be obscure enough if anyone happened to hear it. A couple of other nurses stood outside a patient's room nearby, though they seemed absorbed in their own conversation.

"Right. Well, maybe the four of us can convene this evening and call him."

Grace shook her head slowly. "He's trying to set up a time to talk when General Yarrow can participate. And besides…well, tonight isn't a good time."

Kristine regarded her shrewdly, arms crossed. Her aide was about the same height, but Grace had a sudden sense of being smaller and on the defensive.

"Are you getting together with Dr. Parran?" Kristine asked.

"For dinner," Grace admitted.

"Do you think that's a good idea?"

No! her insides screamed, but she couldn't reveal that to Kristine, nor why. She shrugged noncommittally. "We want to share thoughts about a couple of patients."

"I'll bet. Well, okay. Just let me know what our next step is."

"Sure," Grace said—wishing she knew.

Simon had suggested a family restaurant for dinner—one with a reputation for being very loud and very crowded.

Grace had agreed. After all, no matter how

high the noise level, neither would need to talk loudly for the other to hear.

Even so, the atmosphere wasn't really conducive to having the conversation she knew they each anticipated. So, after they both finished their hamburgers—excellent rare, red meat— she agreed to let him come back to her living quarters. For a while. For a conversation. That was all.

Grace was glad not to see Kristine when they arrived at the building. Nor, fortunately, was her aide around when Simon and she took Tilly for a brief, brisk walk along the paths of the air-force base. Kristine would undoubtedly get the wrong idea about Simon's joining her there.

Interestingly, Tilly seemed to immediately recognize Simon for what he was, sniffing him eagerly, willing to recognize him as alpha when Simon uttered brief commands.

"Nice dog," Simon commented as they returned inside, giving Tilly a pat. The dog wagged her tail in a friendly response.

In her apartment, Grace poured them both beers, then sat on the sofa in her cramped living room across from the rust-colored armchair Simon took. Tilly lay at his feet, causing a momentary irritation in Grace that she immediately quashed. Tilly was simply welcoming a stranger.

Grace took a sip of the cold, pungent brew as she regarded Simon. She decided to take control of the conversation.

"We could play games about this all night," she said. At the amused and suggestive lift of his dark eyebrows, she wished she could take back her words and restate them. Instead, she tamped down her own heated interest and continued, "But I think we should both be honest." Partly. There were things she still couldn't say. "As I said, I saw you shifting a few nights ago, too, Simon. It's always been a sensitive subject between us, one that we never were honest about with one another—before. But here we are. Both of us are shapeshifters. Both of us are werewolves. And, boy, it really feels odd finally admitting that to you."

She smiled tentatively, awaiting his response. He couldn't deny it, but would he embrace the situation or taunt her with it?

He laughed. "That's for sure."

Grace smiled in relief. "Now that's out of the way...well, I have a question for you. When I saw you shift, it wasn't the night of a full moon. How did you do it?" She almost hated to ask, since it gave him tacit permission to ask her, too. But she had to know—even if she couldn't reveal all in return.

His expression tightened. He picked up his glass from the coffee table between them and took a swig of beer. "I knew that was coming. I'll show you mine if you'll show me yours."

It was only fair, Grace knew. But things in this situation weren't exactly even—or fair.

"I'm not sure what your circumstances are, Simon. But I know mine are different from yours." She stared into his curious but suddenly remote golden-brown eyes. "I'm not permitted to tell you anything, but—"

"That's convenient." He shook his head. "Then I guess I'm not 'permitted' either." He paused, then met her gaze directly. "But I'll bet your position is somehow related to your being a military officer, right?"

She sucked in her bottom lip. She had always known how smart Simon was. His perception was no less acute now than when they were in undergraduate school. Maybe even more so.

"Stalemate," she whispered, knowing he heard the word loudly. "For now. But—" She looked at her watch. It was 1930 hours here. That made it 2230 at Ft. Lukman. Late, yes, but she would be surprised if Drew Connell was asleep. "Let me make a phone call, and then I'll know if I can say any more."

When he didn't object, she went into her bed-room where she kept the Alpha Force satellite phone. Tilly followed, and Grace shut the door behind them.

She turned on the aging television across from the queen-size bed where she slept. Simon would probably be able to hear her anyway, so she would have to be careful about what she said—unless she obtained the permission she sought.

The major answered immediately. "Every-thing okay, Grace?"

"Only if you consider my...abilities being found out by another shapeshifter who's not... with us to be okay."

"You're kidding."

"I wish." Not exactly true. But there would be time enough later to explain the complicated circumstances of Grace's non-relationship with Simon. "He's another doctor here at Charles Carder. He can shift outside the full moon, but he won't tell me how unless I tell him. So...do I have your permission, sir?"

"Limited," he snapped. "You obviously can't tell about the actual covert nature of Alpha Force. Just tell him you have access to a special formula that allows you to shift more or less at will—then be sure to learn the source of his ability. Meantime...one of us in authority needs to talk to this guy, but as you can imagine I'm a little preoccupied. I'll speak with Patrick, get him on his way there as soon as possible—maybe tomorrow. I was sending him anyway to discuss our plans for setting up the biohazards thieves. You and he together can have another conversation with this guy. Learn more. Maybe even recruit him into Alpha Force. In fact…you can't tell him what we're about, but why don't you sound him out about joining the military to open all sorts of new vistas to him regarding shapeshifting—but keep it general, no details. Got it?"

"Yes, sir." That would only convince Simon all the more that his surmises about her military affiliation were true. She would have to be careful about how she phrased things. "I'll look forward to seeing Patrick."

She hung up and turned off the T.V. Tilly and she returned to her living room. Simon had made himself at home and had a second beer bottle in front of him. He patted Tilly's head as they got near him. He looked so domestic. Part of Grace's life. Someone she wanted to get close to. Touch. Be touched by…

But that couldn't happen.

"So," he said to Grace, "did your commanding officer give you permission to talk to me?"

Grace closed her eyes and shook her head

slowly. It would make life a lot simpler if Simon were dense or stupid or unaware. But one of the things she loved about him was his intellect and—

Hell. Had she just suggested to herself that she loved him? No way. Bad idea. Years ago, there'd been that chance. Not now.

"Apparently you've made some good guesses, but I can't tell you much, at least not yet. Just know that I have access to a special tonic that allows me in some circumstances to shift without a full moon. There are things in the works that may allow me to be more forthcoming, but that's all I can say at the moment…although I think it's okay to say that, if you'd be interested in joining the military, there would be a lot of benefit to you."

"Join the military? You've got to be kidding." His gaze was suddenly cold and incredulous.

"No," she said, "I'm not." She looked at him, trying to hide the sorrow inside her.

Oh, yes. There was no way she could allow her emotions free rein around Dr. Simon Parran. He apparently disliked the military, which was now an important part of her life. Patrick Worley would probably attempt to recruit Simon—which would likely be impossible.

"Now it's your turn," she continued. "I know

you can do whatever you want, including wait till those circumstances I've mentioned come to fruition, but I'd love to hear how you're able to shift without a full moon."

"That was my goal way back when, Grace, one reason I went to medical school." He stood and approached her, edging around Tilly.

Grace stood, too, waiting for him to draw closer. "Then you figured out a way to control your shifts?"

"Still working on it. I use the downstairs Charles Carder lab facilities now—that's one reason I'm on staff at a military hospital. To the powers-that-be, I'm working on some homeopathic remedies to help infectious-disease patients regain strength. But though I'm far from being finished, I've developed a formula that lets me shift when the moon isn't full—and, on a limited basis, lets me keep my human form during a full moon."

"Really?" Her excitement at what he said caused Grace to blurt out her surprise. She knew her reaction told him something about her abilities, or lack thereof—and therefore the abilities of the military group to which she belonged.

But this was huge. Alpha Force's elixir did not allow control during a full moon, except to help enhance a shifter's human awareness.

Grace felt excitement build within her. She knew that Drew and the other Alpha Force researchers wanted to expand their abilities, and this was one aspect of what they were working on.

They would absolutely want to recruit Simon—or to otherwise obtain access to his research and formula. Would he consider selling it? Working together with Alpha Force without being part of it?

"It's true," he said. "I gather that the stuff you take doesn't do that."

"I wish I could tell you more," she responded dejectedly. "But I can't. Not now, at least."

Not until she got the go-ahead from Drew, who might give Patrick the okay once he'd been here and spoken with Simon.

Things would be so much better if Simon changed his mind. Became part of the wonderful, dedicated military unit to which she belonged.

But she had already experienced Simon's stubbornness once he made up his mind about something. Like refusing to admit his true nature years ago, despite how close they'd gotten. Maybe because of it. He'd stayed secretive then. If she learned more about it now, would she get him to change his mind?

"That's one good reason not to join the military." Simon regarded her as if he could read the frustration circling her mind. "Too much secrecy." He sat down again.

That was ironic, coming from him. "And that from the man who wouldn't admit he was a shifter way back when. But why wouldn't you? Every once in a while, you indicated there was something wrong with your family that kept you from talking to anyone, but wouldn't say what it was, let alone the truth about who you are."

He leaned forward in the chair. "If I tell you about my family, will you be honest with me about your military unit and your shifting abilities?"

"You know that what I can say is limited."

"I figured, but I thought I'd ask. Anyway, there's no reason now not to tell you what happened to my family. Ugly stuff. There were some people who came around. They were from out of town—we never did find out exactly where. They claimed also to be shapeshifters, but they only wanted us to admit that we were. They prided themselves on being hunters of the supposedly supernatural. Some of my relatives were deceived into thinking they were really good guys, shifters like us, and admitted they were shifters, too. Once the creeps were sure, they murdered my aunt and cousin. Of course, thanks to my uncle, they didn't live long enough to gloat about it."

"But the damage was done," Grace said softly. "In so many ways. I'm really sorry, Simon." Even talking about it a lot of years later was clearly painful to him. "It explains so much. The admission of being shifters was what cost your family members their lives. It's totally understandable now why you wouldn't talk about it with someone else—especially someone like me, who tried so hard to get you to admit it. I'm sorry about that, too. And about—"

He rose once more and stood in front of her as Tilly moved out of the way, looking down with those delicious golden eyes that she had come to know so well.

"You didn't know. I didn't let you, then. And now... Now it doesn't matter. We have a lot in common, Grace." He smiled. "And not only because we're shifters."

There was hunger in his gaze. Lust.

She had managed to control the embers of desire that always ignited inside when she was with Simon. But now, her passion flared, as if it had suddenly burst into flame.

Impulsively, she reached up—and was suddenly in Simon's arms.

His lips met hers, claiming them. His tongue

penetrated her mouth, entering into a sexy duel that made her knees weak.

Before she could sink, he lifted her into his arms, his mouth not leaving hers.

"Your phone call was from the bedroom?" he asked.

"Yes," she said and pointed generally toward it, eager for the wonders that awaited her there.

Chapter 14

Simon stayed the night.

His presence filled the small unit that was Grace's Arizona home, especially the small bedroom where the sounds of their lovemaking reverberated against the walls.

His scent was raw and masculine and hypnotic. His body was hard and skilled. His growls and sexy rumbles were as wild as the most feral natures of each of them.

Simon's touch, his taste, his exquisitely intense and erotic lovemaking… Grace's most delightful memories couldn't compare with the reality of spending hours in Simon's embrace, beneath him, surrounding him. Even the sex they had shared briefly only a week or so ago… It had been delicious, but it had been over much too quickly when compared with this captivating, prolonged and extraordinary experience.

When Grace finally fell asleep, she felt sated. Exhausted. And when daylight arrived, Simon only had to touch her gently before they made love all over again.

Finally, clearly spent, his breathing gasping into her ear as they lay in a limp bundle wrapped in her bedclothes, Simon muttered, "I'd better go back to my place and shower and change. No fresh clothes here. Yet."

The possessive suggestion made Grace grin to herself. She turned to burrow her face against the black and silver hairiness of his hard chest.

But she felt her expression shift grimly as reality intruded into her mind.

They had as much in common—more, in many ways—than she had even dreamed of originally.

They also had barriers between them that might never be overcome. Like her commitment, for so many reasons, to the military. To Alpha Force.

But this wasn't the time to talk about that. If nothing else, for the sake of her unit and its success, she had to do all she could to encourage

Simon to share the formula he had created to help control his shifting. She felt certain there'd be some give and take, that he could trade some of his secrets for those of Alpha Force—on a limited basis that only her superior officers could determine. He would benefit from the exchange, too.

She would be his liaison. Would take her lead from Lt. Patrick Worley soon.

Patrick would also help advise about sending pseudo-sick people here to Charles Carder to flush out the biohazards thieves.

And when that was done, when Grace's mission was over and she returned to Ft. Lukman for her next assignment?

This wasn't the time to think about that, either. Instead, she moved her sensitive breasts against Simon's chest as she reached down for him one more time.

"Again?" He definitely sounded interested.

"Again," she confirmed as his body reacted to her touch.

Simon stayed long enough to shower—alone, to prevent any further distractions for now, he said. But he gave her one heck of a kiss before he left. One full of promise and temptation.

When he was gone, Grace hurriedly put on

some clothes and took the very patient Tilly out for a walk in the growing morning heat. The dog had stirred frequently during the night but hadn't interrupted the humans and their strenuous activities on the bed above where she'd slept. Grace praised her now for being such a good girl.

On their way back into the residential building, Grace stopped as Kristine and Bailey caught up with them. The two dogs sniffed noses in greeting as residents in camo uniforms passed by.

"So you're alone now?" Kristine said with a smug smile. She was in casual clothes, and her short, dark hair appeared mussed, as if Bailey and she had been running. "How was your night?"

Grace closed her eyes briefly. When she opened them, she moved aside to allow a couple more people exiting the building to get by. "And you knew I wasn't alone how?"

"I didn't exactly. But I saw the way Simon and you got together in the second-floor kiddy-wing lounge yesterday. The way you looked at each other told me a lot. And since you didn't call to bug me yesterday evening, I figured—"

"It's not exactly what you think," Grace said. "Well, it is and it isn't." She had been considering what, if anything, to tell her fellow Alpha Force members about Patrick's impending visit. She might not reveal much to Autumn and Ruby, but her right hand, Kristine, needed to know at least the essentials.

"That tells me a lot." Kristine jutted her chin characteristically forward as she smiled. "Should I guess what it means?"

"No. Let's walk a little more."

"Bailey and Tilly will like that."

They strolled along the paved pathway from the building. Grace looked around to make sure there weren't any people closeby before she said, "When I shifted two nights ago, Simon saw me."

"What!" Kristine stopped so abruptly that Bailey yanked on his leash, then sat and regarded her reproachfully. She patted him as she spoke. "Oh, damn. What'll we do now? Can we trust him to keep it to himself? Or has he contacted the media already? Did you sleep with him to bribe him, or should we—"

Grace knew her laugh was thin as she raised the hand not holding Tilly's leash. "Not to worry," she said. "He won't say anything. Not if he wants me to keep his secret. I saw him shifting, too, around a week ago."

Kristine looked as if she wanted to slide

down to the pavement and sit for a while. "And you didn't tell me before because...?"

"Because you didn't need to know." And because Grace had wanted to protect him before. Still did, but she was also practical and hoped he'd be convinced to work with Alpha Force, one way or another. "But I've learned he's developed his own chemical formulation to modify the times of his shifts, and it has some aspects that could be useful to Alpha Force. I called Ft. Lukman. Drew, unsurprisingly, is busy, so he's sending Patrick Worley in his place both to talk to Simon and to work with us on how best to stage our outbreak to tempt our thieves with test samples."

"Wow. This is amazing. I'm at a loss for words."

"That's definitely amazing." Grace smiled at her assistant. "And it's all you need to know for now. Ready to go back?"

"Sure." As they again traversed the sand-strewn path between the drought-tolerant vegetation, Kristine was silent for a while. As they reached the door again, the feel of air conditioning wafted out when someone walked out. When those people were outside hearing distance, Kristine said, "And I'm supposed to

believe that Simon and you talked about shapeshifting all night?"

Grace laughed. "Believe what you want. I'm
changing clothes now. Want to walk to the hospital with me in about half an hour?"

"Sure thing."

When Grace and Kristine arrived at the Infectious Diseases Center on the second floor,
the duty nurse, Jen, ran up to them. "Problem,"
she said. "Glad you're here. Some visitors came
in to see one of our PTSD patients, and they
were sick. All of them, apparently. The initial
assessment is MRSA, but we won't know for
sure until lab tests are run. The patient they
visited is showing symptoms already. A couple
of the visitors are family members, and at least
one had been in a local rehab facility and could
have gotten sick there. We've admitted the visitors and have the patient and them in isolation,
but this could be bad."

Grace shared a look with Kristine. Damn
right, this could be bad.

It also could be the way to trap the thieves.

The acronym MRSA stood for "methicillin-
resistant Staphylococcus aureus." In short, it
was a type of staph infection particularly resistant to antibiotics. As far as Grace knew, the
disease wasn't considered a bioterrorist threat.

But in the wrong hands, unchecked, the fluids that contained a particularly bad antibiotic-resistant disease could be used for nasty results.

It was a shame they had no viable suspicions about who the thieves were. But starting rumors around here about how dangerous the stuff was, how it could be a major threat in the wrong hands, might be the way to go. It might even be true.

Grace would call her superior officers soon and alert them. If Patrick was around today or tomorrow to talk about Simon, all the better. He could help supervise their game.

Simon appeared in the hallway beyond Jen then. The sight of him caused Grace's temperature to simmer, but she kept her reactions in check. This was not the time to think about last night.

Simon hurried toward them. "Moe Scoles is down there." He gestured toward the far end of the hall. "He and I gave our current patients their initial checkups of the day. Fortunately, none appeared to have additional symptoms, and standard sanitary practices have already been beefed up. Right now, you and I are assigned to the PTSD wing," he said to Grace, "to check the remaining patients for any symptoms of MRSA. You okay with that?"

He looked deeply into her eyes. She read in

his that, as professional as he was acting, he was genuinely concerned about her.

A pang of warmth surged through her. She smiled back, but grimly. "I'd better be." It wasn't like she could object even if she wanted to. This was a military hospital. She could wait for direct orders, but no need.

"I'll go to the isolation unit to see if there's anything I can do to help there," Kristine said.

"Sounds good," Grace responded. "I'm sure I don't have to tell you to be careful." Or to keep her eyes and ears open, she said silently with a look. Kristine gave a small nod and hurried off. "Let's go," Grace said to Simon.

He handed her a mask and donned one himself as they approached the psychiatric unit. When they entered, Grace made certain that the door locked behind them.

The last time she had been here, a lot of patients and nurses had been clustered together in a lounge to see Tilly do her tricks. Now, no one was visible in the hallway at first. A nurse soon appeared, dashing up to them. She had a mask on, too. "Glad you're here. I don't see any indication of anyone else with symptoms, but after seeing what poor Alice Johns went through…"

That answered one of Grace's questions. She

hadn't heard before which of the PTSD patients was the one who'd been infected.

After scrubbing at a nurses' station to ensure they carried no infection, Simon and she decided to go together to see the remaining patients to make sure they missed no indications of the disease. Since symptoms included red, swollen areas of infection, sometimes pimples oozing pus, at least an initial diagnosis of the possibility of MRSA wasn't hard. Confirmation of the dangerous staph infection was another thing, though. So was initial diagnosis before the sores were apparent.

The smells here were strong, but not of disease, only disinfectants and the odors Grace had experienced in the psych unit before.

The first PTSD patient they saw was Sgt. Jim Kubowski, who'd initially seemed indifferent to Tilly during her first performance but wound up hugging her—and was happy to see her the second time. He hadn't made much of an impression on Grace before, but now the medium-height guy struck her as being very pale beneath his round cheeks. "You going to be able to keep us from getting whatever Alice got?" he asked almost timidly.

"We hope so," Simon replied.

"A friend of mine was a POW for a while. When we got him back, he had this terrible infection. Could be the same thing. They saved him, but no one was sure at first."

"We'll do all we can to make sure Alice and her family members are okay," Simon said in a soothing tone. He was the one to check Kubowski's vitals and ask him questions to elicit a description of any symptoms. Simon also did a check of the guy's skin to look for the sores. He found none, and the guy seemed fine to Grace, too. That's what they noted in his chart.

Despite removing and discarding disposable gloves, they both carefully scrubbed up again before approaching the next patient. It was someone who hadn't been at Tilly's performances. Then they visited PFC George Harper's room. The guy who'd been so warmly accepting of Tilly's presence the first time and a little standoffish the second also appeared fine.

They dropped in on a couple more patients with no indication of the disease, and then they went to Sgt. Norman Ivers's room. Grace wasn't looking forward to this, and she wasn't disappointed. This PTSD patient was just as nasty as he had been for Tilly's first performance.

"Hey, nice to see you, Dr. Andreas," he said in a sarcastic tone. He was lying in his bed in a T-shirt, the sheet pulled up to his waist. His black hair was straggly, and he appeared as if he hadn't shaved for at least a week. "What, no dog this time? I wanted to give that cute little fellow a pat. Or a punch. Whatever."

"This isn't a visit for entertainment," Grace responded. She glanced sideways at Simon, whose hard expression suggested he wanted to give this patient a punch…or whatever. "We're here to make sure you're feeling okay."

"That's right. I hear our dear little Alice had some of her nearest and dearest come in and make her sick—and maybe the rest of the hospital, too. Isn't that a kick?"

She wanted to give him a kick but said very professionally, "Yes, unfortunately there is a possibility of an outbreak of a highly contagious disease. That's why Dr. Parran and I are here. Can you tell us if you have any lesions on your skin, any sores that you didn't—"

"Oh, I'm fine. Otherwise, I'd give you a big hug and kiss so I could pass along the pleasure."

"In that case, I think Dr. Parran will do the honors of checking you over." Not necessarily a good idea, since Simon seemed as revolted by the guy as she felt, but she didn't want to get any nearer to him—and not because she thought he had MRSA or anything else contagious.

Fortunately, or unfortunately, he seemed fine except for the strong smell of the meds used to help ease patients out of addictions. He was their last patient to check in the psychiatric ward, so after making notes on his chart and scrubbing again, Simon and she left.

They returned to the Infectious Diseases Center, where they entered onto the hospital computer system whom they'd seen and that they had found nothing alarming with them.

"Was everything okay?" Jen, the nurse, no longer had her mask on. She looked pale and tired.

"Fine," Simon told her. "Need anything here? Otherwise I'll head over and see what I can do at the isolation ward. I assume Dr. Andreas will stay here to hold down the fort." He looked at her, his expression issuing a command. But Grace wanted to be where she could help most.

Including seeing what kinds of samples were being taken from the affected patients, where they were being tested and stored, and what the plans were for handling and incinerating them.

"You assume wrong, Dr. Parran." Grace shot him a quelling look, then turned to Jen. "Unless, of course, I am needed here." If so, she would stay—for a while.

"I think we're okay. We've a full staff of nurses available, and if we need a physician I'll page you. As long as that's all right."

"That's fine," Grace said. "Let's go, Dr. Parran." Ignoring any objection by Simon, Grace hurried away toward the stairway that would take her down to the E.R., and the isolation ward that sat nearby.

As she neared it, she caught the nauseating odor even before they entered the sealed-off area. The efficient staff had attempted to mask it with disinfectants and other cleaning solutions, but Grace wasn't fooled.

She glanced at Simon, who'd marched silently beside her as if irritated that she hadn't heeded his attempt to protect her.

Nice, heroic thing to do, she supposed. But she had her own agenda, which included complying with her orders from Alpha Force.

Simon clearly caught the smell now, too. His nose was wrinkled in a show of distaste, but not even that detracted from how handsome she found him. Which wasn't necessarily a good thing, even after all they'd shared.

Sure, it was enjoyable. It was also likely to be ephemeral. Again.

"You ready for this?" she asked.

"As ready as you are." His frown deepened. She prepared to say something nasty, making it clear that he was not the boss of her—that she had other bosses, and he now knew that. But before she spoke, he said, "Glad to watch your back here, Lieutenant."

She grinned and headed for the nearest nurses' station to scrub up.

Damn, but he wanted to throttle the stubborn woman. Now that he had learned who and what she was, he wanted to take care of her even more than he had in the past. They shared a lot.

Including a career of treating people with diseases that could kill them—after they'd passed it on to others.

Like the patients inside this area Simon had just entered with Grace. The smell was overwhelming here despite all that had been done to attempt to get rid of it. He'd caught some smells in the psychiatric wing, too, but since they didn't seem related to the new disease outbreak he'd ignored them.

The nurses' station all but blocked anyone who had managed to get in, even with the hospital ID cards that had to be swiped outside and limited access to people with no business in certain areas. The woman behind the desk, Sharon, looked at Grace and him. "Hello, doctors. You here to help?"

"Yes, they are." That was Dr. Moe Scoles, who had come up behind her. "Good thing, too. I think we've contained it, but I don't have to tell either of you the dangers of MRSA. If I'm wrong, this hospital could become a disaster area."

"We won't let it," Grace said. She moved around the desk toward Scoles. "Has MRSA been confirmed? By testing, I mean. I assume specialists like you can recognize what appears to be the lesions it causes."

"Yes, we've collected nasal swabs and sent them downstairs to the lab for culturing. We should get confirmation within twenty-four to forty-eight hours."

"Fine," Simon said. "So what would you like us to do here?"

"Thought you'd never ask. Some of Alice's relatives work at a rehab facility near downtown Phoenix. That's undoubtedly where they started passing around the MRSA infection. We've alerted them, and they've started increasing their precautions against the contagion. They also sent three more infected patients our way who've just arrived. We'll need them checked over and swabbed. If it looks like they've also got MRSA—which they undoubtedly will— they'll need to be introduced to the first regimen of antibiotics."

"Has it worked for the initial group of patients?" Grace asked.

"Looks possible, but you know how resistant MRSA is to treatment."

"Show me which patients need to be examined," Grace said.

Simon knew he wouldn't convince her to let him deal with this. "Show both of us," he told Scoles.

Chapter 15

The rooms in the isolation ward were small—
the better to keep them as sanitized as possible.

Grace was assigned two of the three new
patients. The first was a man in his forties.
He was awake and aware of what was going
on with him, staring at her in her disposable
sanitary mask. "I've heard of this MRSA stuff
before, doctor. I'm an air-force veteran, and was
staying at the rehab facility after follow-up surgery, thanks to a recurrence of problems from
an old injury. Some people came down with
MRSA when I was in the first hospital after
returning to the States, and a bunch didn't sur-

vive." His eyes were worried as he looked at her. "I'll be okay, though, won't I?"

She had already seen the red, pussy lesion on his arm that indicated the possibility of MRSA. She hardly needed to look at it. The smell in this room was ghastly to her heightened senses. "We'll take good care of you." That was the best she could promise, as much as she wanted to swear he'd be fine. With a nurse standing behind her in the doorway, she used her gloved hand to rub the inside of his nose with a swab to obtain a sample. The nurse, also well covered with disposable protective items, collected the swab in a plastic container, which she sealed.

Grace injected the patient with the initial antibiotic, one that sometimes helped to fight off the highly resistant staph infection that was MRSA. If it didn't work, they had others to try. They had to find the right combination to combat this epidemic and save this patient and the others.

When they left the room, Grace watched carefully as the nurse placed the swab-containing vessel, marked with the patient's name, room number and other identifying information, into a larger one.

Both removed their gloves and masks and changed into new lab jackets. The old stuff— even the jacket—was placed in sealed containers to be carefully decontaminated or disposed of. They ran their hands beneath an ultraviolet light to ensure there was no glow—a sign that they had gotten bacteria on themselves.

A similar scenario occurred in the next room. Once again, Grace paid attention to the sample. The large container in which it was placed was the same as the prior one, and it contained a few other sealed capsules. It was large enough to be put onto a gurney where two orderlies, also in sanitary garb, prepared to wheel it downstairs to the lab floor. Grace would have preferred that one of the two people handling the samples be a security guard—possibly armed. But two people were better than one to keep the samples safe. And so far no samples had been stolen while still inside in the hospital—only after being taken outside for disposal.

Besides, having the samples handled this way might be more tempting for the thieves. That could be a good thing. Grace had already notified Autumn and Ruby. But would they be a sufficient force to catch the thieves? For one thing, Kristine, like Grace, was still occupied in the hospital.

When Grace and the nurse finally peeled off the clothing from the second examination, she was approached by Simon.

"Stay back," she said. "I need to shower."

"You okay?" he asked, earning a smile from her.

"I will be. See you on the outside."

The nurse and she headed toward the facilities to disinfect with antibacterial soap and hot water. When Grace emerged in clean aqua hospital scrubs, she hurried out the door from the enclosed ward into a lounge. As she had hoped, Simon was already there. Alone. Grace assumed that word was out about MRSA being diagnosed here at Charles Carder. Visitors would be limited and instructed not to stay long. Precautions would be taken to avoid spreading the highly contagious disease.

"Did the patient you saw likely have MRSA?" she inquired.

"That was my initial diagnosis. Yours, too?"

She nodded. "I was told that Moe Scoles is back in his office. I need to talk to him. I'll see you later."

"I'll come along." His expression was both grim and determined, and it somehow warmed her heart—while at the same time worrying her.

"I'll be discussing security with him," she said. "Military matters. I don't think—"

"Helping to keep things around here safe, or as safe as possible, may be military matters, but

I might be able to contribute something—even though I'm definitely not throwing on any uniform but a medical one."

She didn't appreciate the reminder of the dilemma simmering between them. Even so, she decided to let him join her.

They headed for Captain Scoles's office in the Infectious Diseases Center on the second floor. His door was closed. Grace heard voices inside. Moe had company. Grace identified who it was: Colonel Nelson Otis. She glanced at Simon. He'd heard them, too.

"Better yet," she said. "I'd like both Moe and the colonel to tell me how security will be handled."

Simon raised his dark eyebrows as if justifiably doubtful of their response. "You think they'll tell you?"

"Colonel Otis requested help after usual military resources were unable to stop the thefts," she revealed to Simon without explaining the kind of help they were providing. "That's why my unit was called in. They may think the worst is over. I don't. And for us to help, we need to be kept in the loop."

Grace knocked and opened the door without waiting for an invitation from inside.

Not surprisingly, Moe was behind his desk

and Nelson sat across from him. They both stared toward the door with similar glowers.

"Everything stable with the patients you saw?" Moe demanded.

"For now, at least," Grace confirmed.

"Mine too," said Simon.

"Then I'll talk with you both later," Moe said, clearly dismissing them.

Instead of leaving, Grace walked farther into the room, Simon at her side. She remained standing, ignoring the remaining chair beside Nelson. She half expected the medical facility's commanding officer to give her a direct order to leave. Not that she'd obey—at least for now.

He knew full well that she, as a member of Alpha Force, had special dispensation to do what was necessary to fulfill the covert unit's mission—even if he didn't fully understand how Alpha Force operated.

Ignoring the bad vibes in the room and the clear, if not spoken, wish for them to leave, Grace said, "I'm glad you're both here. Simon and I are concerned about the security of the samples taken from the new patients. I know that confirmation of their nature won't be complete for another twenty-four hours or more. Can I assume then that they'll be handled like the Rocky Mountain spotted fever samples the other day?"

That would be both good and bad. The security employed regarding those samples had worked well to protect them. Possibly too well. Although there could have been other reasons, no one had even attempted to steal them—and therefore put themselves out in the open to be caught.

"No need," Moe said. "Have you ever heard of MRSA being considered as a biohazard that could be used for terrorist warfare? It's not generally given a biohazard rating level. Even the spotted fever materials had a level 3 rating, despite the remoteness of any ability to alter the samples into a transmittable form. Why would any thief go after this stuff?"

"Because in some ways it's more hazardous than some of the diseases that are rated." Simon answered before Grace did. "MRSA spreads fast, and its response to known treatments is dubious."

Grace thought of an even more acerbic retort but kept it to herself. She didn't like Scoles's cavalier attitude. Instead, she turned to the colonel, almost wishing she was in her camo uniform instead of hospital scrubs. This old-school military physician might take her more seriously.

"If nothing else, sir," she said, "we can let it be known that this stuff is dangerous and could be used as biohazards—whether or not that's true. Then, with the right kind of security—" meaning, as he would know, Alpha Force's presence as well as whatever he put into place "—we'll be ready to catch whoever tries to steal it."

The colonel stood. He was big and beefy, and under other circumstances Grace would assume he was attempting to intimidate her. Maybe he even was now. But Simon, despite having no military background, was taller and more muscular, and he placed himself beside her—facing Nelson.

With her own military background and training, Grace felt fully capable of defending herself. Even so, she appreciated Simon's protectiveness.

Nelson approached no closer. "Okay, Grace. Simon. You've made your point. The stuff is in a uniquely precarious situation. The lieutenant and I will discuss with our security expert, Major Dryson, how best to protect it when the time comes to store and dispose of it. We'll treat it as if it is a recognized biohazard."

"And you'll keep me informed about its storage and movement." Grace didn't make it a question as she looked straight into the colonel's eyes. He'd narrowed them so much that they almost sank into the flesh of his chunky face. "I didn't get all the information I should have about the handling of the spotted fever materials."

"That worked out just fine, didn't it?" Moe's tone was scoffing, but she still didn't look at him.

"You know how I can help, colonel," Grace said. Nelson sort of did, at least. He, unlike Moe, knew of the existence of Alpha Force and the reason for its presence here. "If we have any hope of catching whoever it is, we need to see this through."

"We'll keep you informed," the colonel promised.

Simon and she left shortly thereafter.

"Did you believe him?" Simon asked as they walked toward her tiny office.

"Do I look stupid?" she retorted.

A few things now bashed within her mind. She was glad Lt. Patrick Worley was due to arrive soon. Alpha Force no longer had to stage a biohazards alert to flush out the thieves. They had one that was real enough.

She'd just have to make sure that word was out about how dangerous the samples could be—which, unfortunately, might be true.

She'd also have to make sure that she and her other Alpha Force comrades were well prepared to deal with it.

She now feared that the thieves weren't just locals who had been observing the hospital for opportunities, or even negligently hired hospital staff planted here to steal whatever they could for foreign terrorists.

Colonel Nelson Otis had called in military help that had resulted in Alpha Force's presence. Captain Moe Scoles seemed to be a physician dedicated to fighting infection and disease. But both, with their medical backgrounds, would know the differences among which samples collected at the hospital were most able to be cultured into high-risk diseases—or at least be threatening enough to convince nonmedical terrorists of the possibility. And both, with their difficult, scornful and dismissive attitudes... well, Grace couldn't help wondering whether one or both of these men were the robbers they sought.

Two more patients were brought in from the rehab facility with presumed MRSA. Simon was the specialist called in for both, which was exactly what he wanted.

He returned to the isolation unit, calling Grace on the way. He wanted to keep her informed about what was going on, even though she was assigned elsewhere. He would continually observe existing infectious diseases patients for additional symptoms. He'd also be the first physician that nurses would notify if any other medical-center patients evinced signs of MRSA.

He knew Grace would want their positions reversed. Whatever her military group's assignment was here at Charles Carder, he felt sure she believed she was being kept out of the mainstream of the current problem on purpose.

He might have no intention of joining that apparently unusual military unit of hers, but he could cooperate, at least to some extent, for now.

Especially after Grace's hints that her unit had special abilities to help shifters like him achieve the results he had strived for all these years—including better control of the time of a shift. And maybe more, too.

Plus, cooperation would potentially give him more time with Grace before she disappeared from his life. This time it would be her choice, but he had little doubt what she would select, between the military or him. Still, he couldn't dwell on that now.

Simon stayed in the isolation ward just long enough to check in on the two new patients, give them whatever encouragement he could, and obtain nasal swabs for testing.

When he was done scrubbing up after the last visit and checking himself under UV lights for evidence of bacteria, he left the area. There was someplace he needed to go—for more than one reason. He headed to the laboratory area in the medical center's basement.

While there, he checked on the progress of the culturing that was being performed on the samples taken from the first apparent MRSA patients. Some were far enough along that the diagnosis was confirmed.

The lab techs, swathed in protective clothing from head to toe, answered Simon's questions about how long the samples would be retained, and how soon they would be hustled out to be destroyed.

Then, when he was alone in the long, quiet hallway, he ducked into the lab he had adopted for his own use. For cover, he pulled out some of his homeopathic samples, just in case anyone popped in while he was there.

He also grabbed a couple of the pills in the formula he had developed to control shifting.

He had a feeling he would need to use at least one of them soon.

"I still don't have the information I need, Lieutenant." Grace knew she was being formal with Patrick Worley, whom she knew from Ft. Lukman, but he was giving her a hard time.

Sort of.

She stood outside in the rear parking lot of the Charles Carder Medical Center, talking with the lieutenant on her cell phone. Kristine was with her, scowling in sympathy. She wore a different nurse's uniform than the one she'd had on that morning. Like everyone else, she had changed into newly laundered and sanitized clothing each time she visited a MRSA patient.

The heat out here was stifling, but that wasn't a surprise on this late Arizona afternoon. But it was more than the temperature that made Grace's face flush.

"Do you think your plan will work?" Patrick demanded. "I know we were supposed to discuss the protocol we'd put into place for having a bunch of 'sick' folks arrive there and get admitted as patients, but Drew and I have already gotten a preliminary okay from General Yarrow and started recruiting our strike force of pseudo-ailing soldiers. I'll put that on hold if you think this MRSA situation will flush out the thieves."

"No way of knowing for sure, Patrick," Grace said. "You know that. It'll save time if it does, but I need to get a few things set up to give it an adequate try."

And not get either Colonel Otis or Lieutenant Scoles too involved, in case they were the perpetrators they sought. But she didn't want to accuse them to Patrick, or even in Kristine's presence, until she had more than irritation with them to go on. Even at that, she also knew better than wedding herself to her suspicions. She would keep an open mind—and suspect everyone until the true guilty parties were in custody.

Almost everyone, she amended in her thoughts. She no longer suspected Simon— and hoped she hadn't just been manipulated into that opinion. She wished she was with him. His calming presence would help her through this potentially difficult time. But they both had to treat patients now.

"I'm still heading there," Patrick said. "Sounds as if things could boil over before I arrive, but I'll help in whatever way I can. Even in matters that aren't directly related."

Grace translated. Patrick was talking about the revelation Grace had made to Drew about running into another shapeshifter here who might have abilities Alpha Force could use, if some kind of agreement—about recruitment or otherwise—could be reached with him.

"Keep me informed about your ETA," Grace told him. It sounded as if he wouldn't get there till late sometime tomorrow.

That might be plenty of time for him to help deal with any attempt to steal the latest biohazardous materials.

Or not.

Grace and Kristine were back inside the hospital. "Do you think the protocols put into place will keep the MRSA infection from spreading here?" Kristine asked.

"Every prescribed precaution I'm aware of seems to have been instituted," Grace said as they walked through the nearly empty lobby. "Including keeping visitors to a minimum, and ramping up cleaning procedures." Grace stopped near the area containing the stairs and elevator bank and faced Kristine. "But for our purposes, we're going to start some rumors flowing. I want you to make sure everyone you check in on, even other nurses, thinks that the MRSA samples are worse than any of the potentially hazardous materials that have already been stolen from here. I want our thieves to hear that from whatever their usual sources are." That, just in case the perpetrators weren't the two men she considered top suspects. They already knew the biohazard level—or not—of these samples.

"Yes, ma'am." Kristine gave her one of her usual joking salutes. Another nurse in hospital scrubs walked by and shot them a questioning look, which sort of amused Grace. This was, after all, a military hospital, even if not all usual formalities were observed.

"Are you heading back to the Infectious Diseases Center for now?" Grace asked.

"Yes, to do some grunt work—and talk up the biohazard nature of the MRSA samples, like you want. Then I'll go back to the air-force base and take our poor mutts for some exercise. I'll contact Autumn and Ruby, get them off their communications assignments, and let them know what's going on here. I'll suggest that they stimulate those rumors of yours, too."

"Good. Make sure they know that, if all goes as I anticipate, we'll be conducting special Alpha Force maneuvers as soon as I learn that the MRSA samples are about to be moved for disposal." Her assistant nodded, obviously understanding what that meant: Grace and Autumn would be shifting to conduct their part of the surveillance. "Just make sure I can reach you by cell phone at all times."

"You got it, ma'am." Kristine snapped another salute, which made Grace gently punch her arm.

"Don't act smart," she muttered.

"I'm always smart, Grace," she said. "You know that. And ready for anything, just like you."

Grace had completed her last rounds of the day in the Infectious Diseases Center. As an extra precaution, she was checking with the nurses' stations in other hospital units, too. So far, there had been no indications of the spread of MRSA at Charles Carder beyond that one PTSD patient who had caught it from her visitors. Even so, Grace visited the psychiatric ward one more time before leaving for the day.

The nurses there looked exhausted, but they assured Grace that no one had shown any symptoms of the difficult-to-treat staph infection. Sharon, the nurse whom Grace had spoken with before, explained how hard it had been to convince the patients here that they weren't all going to get sick like Alice, even though Grace and the other doctors who'd seen them had said the same thing.

Then it was time for Grace to leave the hospital for the day, but she wasn't ready to go. Her instincts said that things were going to happen soon. Or maybe it was just her wanting to get her mission accomplished.

Besides, she hadn't seen Simon for hours, though she'd thought of him. A lot. As far as she knew, he had remained assigned to the isolation unit. She hoped he was faring well.

Despite all her best instincts, she also hoped she would see him soon.

She didn't want to interfere if he was busy with patients. On the other hand, maybe she could help.

Fortunately, they had exchanged cell phone numbers.

She sent him a text message: All ok?

The response was quick: Meet me in pkg lot.

She did. She was relieved to see that, although there was exhaustion in his eyes, he looked well and alert.

And, somehow, jazzed.

He smiled as he approached her. She saw his hands flex, then fall back to his sides, as if he had wanted to embrace her—which only made her own instinct flare into a desire to hold him, too. But she just waited.

He bent down and said softly into her ear, "Just heard. The samples from all but the latest patients have been cultured and analyzed. Yes, it's MRSA. And the samples will be disposed of tonight."

Chapter 16

Once again, Grace stood with Kristine in the shadows at the far side of the parking lot, both in dark clothing, both on alert. Grace was even more primed this time than the last—maybe because the last time she had attempted to foil the bad guys, they'd played hooky. She doubted they would tonight.

Unless all the rumors she had started, and gotten others to spread, failed to excite the thieves into believing they were about to score a huge heist of dangerous biohazards, they'd be there.

Even doctors—like Nelson Otis and Moe Scoles—might like to pick up these biohazardous materials, if they were the thieves. And they, of course, would believe they knew all the security measures in place.

Like Dryson's security guys. She would have to be careful not to get in their way—or allow them to get in hers. She would probably scare them.

She would be in wolf form.

Simon wouldn't. She'd had a talk with him. As hard as it had been to stay remote and formal in his presence—when she had wanted to throw herself into his arms—she had merely thanked him for his help. Told him that she and the other military folks, especially those in Alpha Force, had things covered tonight. No civilian assistance was needed. He was not to put himself in harm's way—in either form.

He had protested. Insisted that he had wanted not only to catch the bad guys, but to watch over her. Despite the warm glow inside her, she'd told him that his shifting could put them both in more danger. It would be easier for one wolf to hide, notwithstanding the security measures near the storage and incineration building. Two would be even more obvious. Kristine was bringing Bailey later, and if another canine was seen, they could claim it was Tilly. But still another?

Because of the acts Grace might perform

while shifted, and despite the extra guards in the vicinity, Autumn and Ruby had managed to perform their magic again on the security cameras, limiting their views so they would not rotate low enough to spot a canine. If the bad guys showed up, as anticipated, they wouldn't be able to crawl on their stomachs even if they wanted to, to elude detection—not if they carried biohazards containers.

Grace and Kristine might be visible on the cameras now, but that was okay. If Colonel Otis paid attention, he would figure they were on duty, performing their Alpha Force function, whatever it was.

Now, after doing a quick preliminary recon, Grace beckoned for Kristine to follow her to the same location along the border of the hospital property and air-force base where she had shifted before. Once again hidden by hedges and ignoring the smell of jet fuel, Grace removed her clothes. She couldn't help glancing around briefly. Last time she'd been here, putting clothes on instead, Simon had been watching her.

Would he keep his promise and stay out of this situation, let those with the responsibility take care of it?

She hoped so, for his sake. And hers. If this situation had the result she wanted, she would be through here. Leaving the hospital. Leaving Simon. Even so, she wanted him to stay safe.

But Simon had never done as she had asked in the past. She wasn't sure he would now.

"Ready?" Kristine whispered.

Grace nodded, and Kristine handed her the Alpha Force elixir, then bent to get the light ready. As Grace downed the potion, she thought fleetingly of Simon again. What was his method, his formula, for shifting when he did?

She didn't have much time to ponder that. Kristine shone the light on her and waited.

In moments, Grace felt the beginning of her shift. Her limbs tightened, her insides changed, and she experienced the inevitable sensations of stretching and discomfort.

"I'll go get Bailey now," Kristine whispered from beside her. "We'll have your back."

That was the last thing Grace heard before no vestige of her human form remained.

Softly, quietly, she crept toward the area where she could remain behind the cover of automobiles and watch the location of interest.

She was glad when the sharp smell of jet fuel segued into the somewhat softer smell of gasoline amid disinfectant aromas emanating from the nearby hospital building.

The pavement was warm beneath the pads of her feet, but not painfully hot now that the sun was down. The parking lot was illuminated by overhead lighting.

She stopped and waited. Hearing the soft sound of wings, she glanced up. A hawk landed on one of the light posts.

There were voices from the far side of the parking lot, closest to the hospital entrance. She moved farther away, positioning herself where she could watch the critical areas in the building where the MRSA samples would be taken.

She sensed additional movement on the fringes of the parking lot. She lifted her nose into the air. Kristine was there, with Bailey. Ruby, Autumn's backup, was there as well.

Grace wasn't alone, although her path to resolve this would be different from theirs.

She crept forward once more, keeping herself far from visibility from the building—and inhaled another scent. She stopped. Growled softly not in anger, but in frustration.

She smelled Simon. At least it was his human scent, but he had gone back on his promise.

She could do nothing about it, but would have to be careful not to let his presence distract her. She had to concentrate on what was bound to occur—

There. It was beginning. Like the last time, when she had watched in human form, two humans wearing sterile clothing exited the tunnel from the hospital, each carrying large containers of what must be biohazard samples. Others were with them—two men in camo uniforms, wielding weapons, plus a third who also appeared wary but did not aim any gun. Was that Major Dryson?

The door to the room where the building's security staff was stationed opened, and the five walked in. The door closed behind them.

Only...she suddenly smelled the terrible yet light chemical stench she had experienced before from that office, when the biohazardous materials were stolen. The door opened once more.

The two men in uniforms dashed out. They carried the containers of hazard samples, strapped somehow around their necks so they could still aim their weapons. They slammed the door shut behind them and started to run.

The guards...they were the thieves!

She looked up to see the hawk circling. The tangos' whereabouts would at least be observed.

But it was time also for her to act.

She was not the only one to hurry forward, dashing through the parking lot among the cars. The other Alpha Force members—those who were not shifters—were to her right, ducking from one area of concealment to the next, as she was doing.

Kristine and Ruby, weapons drawn and ready to fire, followed the thieves, saying nothing yet but ready to take them down. Bailey, his leash attached to a belt at Kristine's waist, loped at her side.

The two men ran toward the back of the storage building, through that portion of the parking lot, and up to the fence that separated the hospital property from the air-force base. The gate there should be locked. They would be trapped.

As they reached it, they turned as if to ensure that no one followed—and one of them spotted the humans behind them.

With no warning, he aimed his weapon and fired.

Kristine fell to the ground.

Damn! Kristine Norwood was shot. Simon watched as the woman with her grabbed the dog's leash while kneeling beside the fallen woman.

Simon hadn't been at all happy about Grace's demands that he stay out of their operation to trap the biohazards thieves.

That was why he partially ignored what he had promised her. He hadn't shifted…yet. He had understood her concern about two roaming wolves being in the area at the same time, and whether that would be more obvious than one. Just because they had both shifted previously at the same time didn't mean they could easily get by with it again.

He'd decided to observe what occurred as a human—unless shifting became, in his estimation, necessary.

He wasn't military. Didn't want to be military. But as a doctor, he knew well what a disaster caused by loosing biological weapons could do.

Was the MRSA virus capable of being used that way? Just because it hadn't been officially recognized as an item of warfare didn't mean it couldn't be weaponized and used to infect masses of people. With its resistance to most antibiotics, it might do a lot of damage.

Had those trying to catch the thieves filled the containers with something benign instead of MRSA materials? Maybe, but no one had known who the bad guys were. They might have been aware of any switch.

Now it seemed apparent that the men they were after were part of the military security team. They would know the capabilities of the others after them.

Most of the others.

Could Simon do something more to help in wolf form now that a member of Grace's team assigned to stop the thefts had been shot? He didn't know if Kristine was still alive, but presumably the other woman with her was doing everything possible to save her. As a doctor, he might be able to help, but that other woman surely carried a cell phone, could call 911 and get help from the ER there stat.

He had other skills that might be more useful now in saving not just one life, but potentially hundreds...or more.

Not to mention the woman—wolf—he cared about so deeply.

He hurried away from the cars that he'd been hiding behind. Sped toward a thick grove of well-watered hedges, out of the line of sight of any person who might be in the parking lot, too.

Once well-hidden, he reached into his pocket and extracted a small plastic bottle that contained one pill.

He placed it far back in his mouth, made himself salivate...and swallowed.

She could do nothing to help Kristine now. Not while shifted. She had to follow the two miserable culprits.

All her instincts while in this form urged her to attack. But the formula that allowed her to shift maintained her human rationality.

She took one further glance around the car that obscured her from view from the building. Help had arrived for Kristine, who was moving. She was alive. She had worn a vest beneath her dark clothing. With luck, she had been struck there. She would feel pain, but she would survive.

The emergency workers and Ruby Belmont were not the only ones with her. Doctors were there too, including the ones she had suspected of being the thieves after they had minimized the importance of the last episode and this one. Colonel Nelson Otis and Captain Moe Scoles were helping to care for Kristine.

Who were the thieves?

She would learn. Now.

Human security forces had converged from the hospital and the tunnel and dispersed, some heading in the right direction though they clearly did not know where the thieves had gone. Grace would need to be cautious to stay out of their way.

Ruby, Autumn's assistant, held Bailey's leash. She had backed away from Kristine. She glanced up to where the hawk circled more widely, and off toward the north, the way the thieves had gone.

Good.

Grace dashed off in the direction in which they had run. Her enhanced senses would allow her to locate them. Autumn's observation from overhead would help.

The perpetrators veered toward the east. That was what the sounds of their running, and the movement of the hawk, indicated. Did any human military members pursuing them go in that direction, too? Grace didn't think so. As far as she could tell, they remained headed west, following what they would consider to be logic. Not using any special senses that enhanced tracking abilities.

But as Grace cautiously yet quickly darted toward the thieves, she realized she was no longer alone. By scent and by sight, she recognized her new pack member who suddenly ran by her side.

Simon.

He glanced toward her, a sleek, silver and black wolf with the glittering eyes of a being as determined as she was.

Together, they would hunt, and bring down, their prey.

The cover of the rows of automobiles ended. Grace stopped, looking in the direction the thieves had gone. Only a line of hedges along the fencing between hospital grounds and the air-force base was there. Where were the objects of their pursuit?

The hawk now circled the edge of the air-force base. Somehow, the humans had gotten through.

Therefore, the wolves would, too.

Glancing around, nose in the air, Grace made as certain as possible that no human pursuers were nearby, then loped toward the barrier. Their prey had obviously touched the plants and wire, had left their scent behind on them.

Simon pushed his muzzle through the growth. There was indeed a hole in the fencing behind it.

The thieves must know this area well, had probably made the hole with wire cutters or otherwise ahead of time. Had possibly used this exit in prior thefts, as well.

Simon shoved Grace out of the way with his body, preceding her through the hole. Was he acting on instinct to try to be alpha of this pack, or had whatever he used to shift also allowed him to maintain some sense of humanity, keeping her from going first, headlong, perhaps, into danger? She liked it, while at the same time feeling anger. He had promised to stay out of danger. She was the military member. She should go first.

But when she got through the opening, he was fine. No one awaited. No guns were fired at them.

They were at the far end of an airfield, close to a row of hangars where planes were stored and repaired.

Where were the men they pursued?

She listened and scented the air as Simon did the same. Simultaneously, they sprinted toward a building in the middle.

The sliding metal door was slightly ajar. Grace heard running footsteps inside. She pressed her nose through the opening before Simon could interfere, saw nothing except a large, looming fighter jet parked there and edged inside. Simon followed.

It was dark in the hangar, with no illumination from the blackened sky outside. Whatever the moon's current angle, it was not now visible. In the distance, Grace saw the faint beam from a flashlight. Moving sideways so her body met the smooth furriness of Simon's, she nodded in that direction.

Together, slowly, carefully, their paws making little sound on the concrete floor, they headed that way.

The two men had entered a small storage

room at the end of the hangar. They turned on the lights.

The men were Sgt. Norman Ivers and Sgt. Jim Kubowski—two of the PTSD patients. Kubowski had seemed like a nice enough guy, for a psych patient. Ivers had been a jerk. But Grace hadn't suspected either. How had they left the psychiatric wing of the hospital without anyone knowing? Why were they stealing the biohazards? Were they enemy agents under cover? If so, why did they allow themselves to be confined at a military hospital—to collect hazardous materials until someone could come for them?

There were cabinets along the wall. One man reached into his pocket and pulled out a key.

Inside the cabinets were shelves filled with cans of oil. Quickly, the men removed them— and pulled out the shelves. Then vertical panels comprising the wall. It was a façade—and behind it was another, deeper, similar set of shelves.

Several were full of containers similar to the one Ivers had carried, then put down on the floor beside him.

Grace had seen enough. Time for human assistance.

But the men spotted them.

"What the hell?" Kubowski shouted. "Did someone set search dogs on us? Let's get rid of them." He pulled a gun from his belt and aimed at Grace.

Before she could react, Simon had raced toward the man. He bit down on his gun hand. The gun went off, the shot going wild, hitting no one.

Grace took no time to react, attacking Ivers to ensure he didn't shoot Simon.

The men fought back, but they were no match for the two angry wolves. They were soon on their backs on the floor, weapons dropped, sharp teeth at their throats.

"Don't move!" shouted a loud, familiar female voice. Grace turned her head to see Ruby standing there, her service weapon drawn and aiming toward the humans. At her side, Bailey was straining at the leash attached now to her belt, obviously wanting to attack the bad guys. He had worked with Grace in this form before. He might go after Simon, though, so it was best that Ruby keep him restrained.

After helping Kristine, Ruby had obviously followed her shapeshifting charge, and Autumn had directed her, too, toward this building.

Human help had arrived.

Grace moved quickly away from Ivers and saw Simon do the same with Kubowski.

Ruby, still aiming at the men on the ground, spoke their location into a radio.

The men didn't move.

"You two had better go," Ruby said, clearly recognizing, despite never having been told, that the canine that was Simon was an ally.

Grace glanced toward the handsome wolf that was Simon. Met his gaze. Nodded.

It was over.

Chapter 17

Sitting on one of the usual hard chairs at a table in the Charles Carder cafeteria—alone—Simon drank coffee and reviewed patient files on his laptop. That way, he avoided looking at anyone around him. The place wasn't crowded, since visitors hadn't yet been welcomed back. Even so, it was noisy, thanks to the few brave souls from outside who were here, plus hospital staff members. It smelled of the usual mediocre food and the people eating it.

Simon was not happy.

Well, not exactly true. He had helped to accomplish what had needed to be done: Catch and stop the thieves.

He had also helped Grace accomplish her mission. And made sure she came through it without being harmed. Although he doubted she would acknowledge his help. She had thanked him last night after they had both shifted back into human form. But since then she had avoided him.

He didn't want to admit it to himself, but that hurt like hell, especially after what they had been through together.

But he couldn't complain. In fact, he was glad about what they had achieved. Not only had they caught the bad guys, but the big bonus was that they had also located all the missing biohazardous materials. The Air Force Security Forces were checking the containers and confirming everything was there—under the direction of their commanding officer here, Major Louis Dryson.

Dryson had thrown himself into the situation by accompanying the movement of the biohazards samples to the storage and incineration building, and had become a victim of the thieves just as his security force stationed there had been. Another chemical had been released that had knocked them out, but all were recuperating. Another good thing.

Simon took another sip of coffee, shaking his head. He should feel good. Everything was wonderful. No one other than Grace and the members of her military group knew that he was a werewolf in disguise, and they would never reveal it to anyone. He had the same knowledge to hang over their heads.

Hell. Enough feeling sorry for himself. Time to go back to work. See some patients—including checking on the MRSA patients whose serious illnesses had triggered this last situation that had ended so favorably.

He closed his laptop and glanced around at the crowd. Some nurses he recognized were just entering the cafeteria. A few more visitors now occupied tables. No one paid attention to him, which was as it should be.

He stood.

"I thought I'd find you here." The familiar, melodic feminine voice from behind him made him smile. He quickly returned his face to the friendly detached expression that he used around most patients.

He'd let himself get preoccupied by feeling sorry for himself. Otherwise, he'd have picked up Grace's scent long before she got so close— softly floral tinged with that intriguing harsher overlay.

He turned. "Hi, Grace," he said, as remotely as if they were strictly uninvolved coworkers.

"Hi." She looked up at him, her sable-brown

eyes both quizzical and—was that sympathy in them? Damn! He didn't want her sympathy for any reason—and he could only guess her rationale.

She undoubtedly was leaving, now that her mission was accomplished. She probably wouldn't even give him the satisfaction of wrapping up loose ends—like explaining what those two psychiatric lunatics had intended by stealing biohazardous materials. How they had managed to do so, and hide the stuff, for so long. Assuming her military cohorts and she had figured all that out.

She ran a hand through her short, silvery blond hair, as if unsure what to do next. He wished he could touch that lovely, familiar hair, too. Grace pursed her lips—which only tempted him even more to kiss them.

"You look so…angry, Simon. I'm sorry, but I don't even know what to be sorry about. But—look, I came here because I'd like you to come with me. Now. For a meeting. An officer in charge of my unit, Alpha Force, has arrived. I'd like to introduce you. We'll be able to tell you some of what we learned about the thieves, Kubowski and Ivers. And… Well, we'll discuss a few other things, if you're willing. Will you come with me?"

Hell, yes, his mind shouted. He had a thousand questions.

Not the least of which were: *Are you disappearing from my life this time, like I disappeared from yours before?*

And: *Will you have sex with me again now? Later?*

And: *What is your military force all about? How did you find a bunch of other shifters like that? Can I continue to trust them to keep my secrets, the way they keep their own?*

But the things he wanted to know couldn't be discussed in front of her commanding officer. Even so, if he didn't go with her now, this would probably be it between them. Forever.

"Sure." He tried to sound offhanded. "Let's go talk to your officer in charge."

Colonel Otis's office was palatial compared with Grace's tiny room at the hospital. It contained plenty of space for the meeting about to be held there. Enough chairs, too, to accommodate the colonel, Captain Moe Scoles, Simon and the five Alpha Force members who were present—the four posted there, plus Lt. Patrick Worley, who had arrived that morning only hours after the apprehending of the biohazards thieves.

Now they all sat around the colonel's desk,

waiting for him to get off the phone and begin their discussion.

When Patrick arrived, he had immediately called a meeting with Grace and the others from Alpha Force, and had monopolized her time with his debriefing in her residential quarters. That meant she hadn't been able to get together with Simon until now.

On their walk here from the cafeteria, she hadn't tried to talk to him about anything except generalities. He'd acted as if they were friendly strangers.

He had distanced himself from her already.

She hadn't hidden that she would be leaving soon, now that her mission here was resolved. But his immediate remoteness hurt as if she had been stabbed with a dagger that could not be removed without doing worse damage than leaving it in.

She hadn't given up on being able to talk him into some cooperation that would allow them at least a little contact in the future. But her sinking heart knew already how receptive he would be to that.

At least she had gotten Patrick off by himself for a few minutes after the Alpha Force conclave for an additional debriefing…about Simon. Patrick was tall, with clipped, light hair and a cleft chin. Although a physician, he wore a camo uniform rather than hospital garb. He was well aware of all that Major Drew Connell knew. But Grace wanted to update her commanding officers with the additional information she had learned. It would be wise for Alpha Force to back her up in getting Simon's cooperation. Or even to keep her out of whatever negotiation they did with Simon, if that resulted in his agreeing to some degree of collaboration.

"Sorry." Nelson hung up the phone. "That was Major Dryson. His Air Force Security Forces have been interrogating the men in custody for the thefts, and he wanted to tell me the latest so I could update you with the information that isn't classified." He looked directly at Patrick as he spoke, as if he would feel more comfortable relaying the message only to another military officer in charge.

"That would be greatly appreciated, Colonel," Patrick said. "I'm eager to hear why some PTSD patients were even motivated to steal the stuff, let alone how they got away with it."

The colonel glowered, as if Patrick had accused him of ineptitude.

"I doubt I'd have suspected them, either," Patrick added, obviously to smooth any ruffled feathers.

Apparently mollified, Nelson began to relate the current understanding of what had happened. Ivers and Kubowski had been overseas in Afghanistan together. While on their tours of duty in Special Forces units, they'd both taken drugs to stay awake, and became addicts. That was part of the reason they had been hospitalized at Charles Carder, for physical issues as well as mental. Both experienced post-traumatic stress disorder as a result of their intense combat experiences. They had not yet been completely weaned from the drugs, and the substances they were on caused paranoia and hallucinations.

While they were overseas some of their comrades were killed by a virulent strain of a highly contagious disease when the enemy loosed biohazardous materials on their outpost. Plus, there had been the situation that Kubowski had revealed to Grace, when a friend had been a POW and returned with a bad infection that, fortunately, had been contained and hadn't proven fatal—but could have.

Then, during their hospitalization back in the U.S., they heard of outbreaks of certain serious diseases in and around Charles Carder. As a result of their experiences, they had believed that the initial biohazard specimens were not being disposed of but were being taken by an enemy and stored for development of biological WMD—weapons of mass destruction.

As a result, they collaborated together, using methods learned while in Special Forces, to escape when they wanted and to elude detection as they left the psychiatric wing, as well as to counter security, including cameras. They were skilled in the arts of disguise and blending in with those expected to wander the area. Plus, they had been schooled in using certain chemicals to render enemies unconscious.

Ivers had previously been stationed at Zimmer Air Force Base and knew its facilities—including where to find some of those chemicals. When Kubowski and he stole the materials, he knew where they could be locked into a storage area that they had managed to physically alter without detection. They considered eventually using the biohazards they collected against enemies of the United States, who, in their deranged state, they believed could even be members of the U.S. military.

"Partly thanks to Alpha Force, we've stopped them." The colonel's acknowledgment sounded somewhat begrudging to Grace. It also didn't give her unit enough credit.

Patrick just nodded. "Are the men still in the military?"

"That's right," the colonel said. "They're subject to courts-martial."

"But if they're as psychologically challenged

as they appear," Patrick countered, "they may get off with just continued hospitalization—in a mental facility without a real hospital attached."

"Unfortunately, that's true."

The audience with Colonel Otis ended a short while later. So, Grace feared, did her proximity to Simon.

But as the Alpha Force members all walked down the hall along with Simon, leaving Moe Scoles in the office with Nelson, Patrick stopped in a small, empty lounge.

He looked at Simon. "This isn't the place to go into any detail, but I'm aware of the degree of help you provided last night. The kind of help, too. In the interest of national security, I'll need to work out certain confidentiality issues with you. First, though—well, I've worked on certain…let's say formulations that you might find of interest, just as I'm interested in what you've been working on. I'd like to present you with a demonstration of ours tonight. Want to give it a try?"

Watching Simon's reaction, Grace held her breath. He had always been so solitary. So independent. Would this be enough to entice him to at least consider working with Alpha Force?

He looked at her. His solemn expression suddenly lightened. He even smiled, causing her insides to somersault in a warm tumble of hope.

"Yes, I'd like that," he said. "As long as Grace joins me."

He loped beside his mate through the desert beyond human fences. The night air was warm, the sand cool and coarse beneath the pads of his feet.

When he looked up, he saw that only half the moon was lighted, a bowl-shaped celestial object, weeks away from being full.

A similarly intense light to the full moon, though artificial, had been used to help initiate his change. That and the liquid formula he had drunk.

He was very aware now of the humanity within him. The knowledge, the intelligence, the sensitivity were all enhanced, so much more than when he shifted with his own formula.

He had told the people involved—Grace, Patrick Worley, the three other Alpha Force women—how his formula allowed him to choose not to shift during a full moon. He admitted it was far from perfect, but they had been impressed, since their Alpha Force did not have that capability at all...yet.

He ran on awhile longer, the female wolf beside him easily keeping up. If he worked things right when back in human form, he would be able to run with her like this often after shifting.

The thought pleased him enough that he instinctively wanted to stop and howl beneath the half moon. But he didn't. Instead, it was soon time to prepare to change back. That was a good thing, for he would then be able to prepare for this future he wanted to achieve.

With Grace.

They had changed back nearly simultaneously. The planning for this shift had been perfect, and they both resumed human shape exactly where their clothing had been left.

This time, Grace's assistant Kristine had been told to go back to their residential units and care for the dogs. Simon and she would watch each others' backs.

"Too bad we can't be sure no one will see us here," Simon said.

Uneasy, Grace quickly donned her underwear. "What do you mean? Is someone around here? Were we observed?"

"Not that I'm aware of," he said. "I'm the one doing the observing, and I definitely like what I see."

He had pulled on his briefs, but before Grace

could grab any more of her clothing he took her into his arms.

His warmth and hardness against her gave her visions of hot, mindless sex...the kind they had already shared. She melted against him, knowing she was probably being foolish. Continuing to hope he would somehow remain in her life could only hurt her even more.

"Let's go to my place," he whispered into her ear. "I don't want to run into any of your cohorts tonight. Tomorrow will be soon enough."

"Soon enough for what?"

"Soon enough for me to tell your buddy Patrick that we need to work out some details."

"For...?" she prompted, holding her breath as she stared up into Simon's golden-brown eyes. He was grinning.

He was teasing her. In more ways than one, since his hardness was growing against her middle as he held her tightly.

"For me to enlist in the military and join your Alpha Force."

"Really?" Grace almost squealed in delight. She held him even tighter, if that was possible, kissing his mouth until he bent farther and met her mouth with his searching, scorching lips.

He pulled away again, but not far. "Yes, really. I'll share the parts of my shifting formula that they need if they let me work with them, participate in experiments, have it all. That was one great shift before. Especially since it was with you—and we weren't chasing bad guys. I also feel better now than I usually do after a shift I created artificially—for many reasons."

"Then you'll really join Alpha Force?"

"I'm not great at taking orders," he warned.

"Tell me something I don't know." She put her cheeks against the warm flesh of his still bare chest, reveling in the feel of having him so close. And in the realization that her hope to keep him in her life just might come true.

"I'll tell you a lot you don't know, as long as you give me time. We'll have the rest of our lives to learn about each other—if you're okay with that."

She drew in her breath. "Are you proposing to me?"

He laughed. "Not yet. That'll come, when we're not practically in the nude in the middle of nowhere, and I have a ring to give you. Meantime, I will tell you something you don't know. After all that happened before, I didn't tell you everything about my family. I happen to have a brother who is also a shifter—werewolf, like me. His name is Quinn Parran, and he's a private investigator. I've shared my formula with him, such as it is, and I might be able to get him to join your Alpha Force if we combine our medicines."

"I'd like to meet him," Grace said.

"He'll like to meet you, too. I told him a lot about you years ago. He'll be surprised about how things are working out between us, and with your military group. Of course I'm surprised, too."

"As am I," Grace said. "But I couldn't be happier."

She reached up once more to give him a kiss that promised, soon, to seal the deal between them…forever.

* * * * *

nocturne™

COMING NEXT MONTH

Available August 30, 2011

#119 LORD OF THE VAMPIRES
Royal House of Shadows
Gena Showalter

#120 THE SHADOW WOLF
Bonnie Vanak

REQUEST YOUR FREE BOOKS!

2 FREE NOVELS FROM THE PARANORMAL ROMANCE COLLECTION PLUS 2 FREE GIFTS!

YES! Please send me 2 FREE novels from the Paranormal Romance Collection and my 2 FREE gifts (gifts are worth about $10). After receiving them, if I don't wish to receive any more books, I can return the shipping statement marked "cancel." If I don't cancel, I will receive 4 brand-new novels every month and be billed just $21.42 in the U.S. or $23.46 in Canada. That's a saving of at least 21% off the cover price of all 4 books. It's quite a bargain! Shipping and handling is just 50¢ per book in the U.S. and 75¢ per book in Canada.* I understand that accepting the 2 free books and gifts places me under no obligation to buy anything. I can always return a shipment and cancel at any time. Even if I never buy another book, the two free books and gifts are mine to keep forever.

237/337 HDN FEL2

Name _____ (PLEASE PRINT)

Address _____ Apt. #

City _____ State/Prov. _____ Zip/Postal Code

Signature (if under 18, a parent or guardian must sign)

Mail to the Reader Service:
IN U.S.A.: P.O. Box 1867, Buffalo, NY 14240-1867
IN CANADA: P.O. Box 609, Fort Erie, Ontario L2A 5X3

Not valid for current subscribers to the Paranormal Romance Collection or Harlequin® Nocturne™ books.

Want to try two free books from another line?
Call 1-800-873-8635 or visit www.ReaderService.com.

* Terms and prices subject to change without notice. Prices do not include applicable taxes. Sales tax applicable in N.Y. Canadian residents will be charged applicable taxes. Offer not valid in Quebec. This offer is limited to one order per household. All orders subject to credit approval. Credit or debit balances in a customer's account(s) may be offset by any other outstanding balance owed by or to the customer. Please allow 4 to 6 weeks for delivery. Offer available while quantities last.

Your Privacy—The Reader Service is committed to protecting your privacy. Our Privacy Policy is available online at www.ReaderService.com or upon request from the Reader Service.

We make a portion of our mailing list available to reputable third parties that offer products we believe may interest you. If you prefer that we not exchange your name with third parties, or if you wish to clarify or modify your communication preferences, please visit us at www.ReaderService.com/consumerschoice or write to us at Reader Service Preference Service, P.O. Box 9062, Buffalo, NY 14269. Include your complete name and address.

New York Times *and* USA TODAY *bestselling author*
Maya Banks presents a brand-new miniseries

PREGNANCY & PASSION

When four irresistible tycoons face
the consequences of temptation.

Book 1—ENTICED BY HIS FORGOTTEN LOVER

Available September 2011 from Harlequin® Desire®!

Rafael de Luca had been in bad situations before. A crowded
ballroom could never make him sweat.

These people would never know that he had no memory
of any of them.

He surveyed the party with grim tolerance, searching for
the source of his unease.

At first his gaze flickered past her, but he yanked his attention back to a woman across the room. Her stare bored
holes through him. Unflinching and steady, even when his
eyes locked with hers.

Petite, even in heels, she had a creamy olive complexion.
A wealth of inky-black curls cascaded over her shoulders
and her eyes were equally dark.

She looked at him as if she'd already judged him and
found him lacking. He'd never seen her before in his life.
Or had he?

He cursed the gaping hole in his memory. He'd been
diagnosed with selective amnesia after his accident four
months ago. Which seemed like complete and utter bull.
No one got amnesia except hysterical women in bad soap
operas.

With a smile, he disengaged himself from the group

around him and made his way to the mystery woman.

She wasn't coy. She stared straight at him as he approached, her chin thrust upward in defiance.

"Excuse me, but have we met?" he asked in his smoothest voice.

His gaze moved over the generous swell of her breasts pushed up by the empire waist of her black cocktail dress.

When he glanced back up at her face, he saw fury in her eyes.

"Have we *met?*" Her voice was barely a whisper, but he felt each word like the crack of a whip.

Before he could process her response, she nailed him with a right hook. He stumbled back, holding his nose.

One of his guards stepped between Rafe and the woman, accidentally sending her to one knee. Her hand flew to the folds of her dress.

It was then, as she cupped her belly, that the realization hit him. She was pregnant.

Her eyes flashing, she turned and ran down the marble hallway.

Rafael ran after her. He burst from the hotel lobby, and saw two shoes sparkling in the moonlight, twinkling at him.

He blew out his breath in frustration and then shoved the pair of sparkly, ultrafeminine heels at his head of security.

"Find the woman who wore these shoes."

Will Rafael find his mystery woman?
Find out in Maya Banks's passionate new novel
ENTICED BY HIS FORGOTTEN LOVER
Available September 2011 from Harlequin® Desire®!

Harlequin®

ROMANTIC
SUSPENSE

NEW YORK TIMES BESTSELLING AUTHOR
RACHEL LEE

The Rescue Pilot

Time is running out…

Desperate to help her ailing sister, Rory is determined
to get Cait the necessary treatment to help her fight
a devastating disease. A cross-country trip turns into
a fight for survival in more ways than one when their plane
encounters trouble. Can Rory trust pilot Chase Dakota
with their lives, and possibly her heart?

**Look for this heart-stopping romance in September
from *New York Times* bestselling author Rachel Lee
and Harlequin Romantic Suspense!**

Available in September wherever books are sold!

www.Harlequin.com.

RSRL27741